Sea

A Stranded Novel

By Theresa Shaver

Author's Note

About Boats

To anyone who has sailed a boat, rode on a boat, read about boats or even looked at a boat...Stop yelling at meeee! I did so much research on the proper terminology for all things sailboat (Oh my aching head). Sat down and wrote away. It was all "bow, stern, fore, aft"...and so on. Then I read it (Oh my aching head)! It was way too much and really took away from the story so I got rid of it and wrote it like a teenager that had never been on a boat before. So I know that some of it was vague but it just sounded better! The time frame used in the story is also not quite accurate. It would take much longer to make that voyage but I had a time frame in mind so I changed it. As the song goes... "It's my party and I'll (write) if I want too." LOL!

About Reviews

I can't even begin to tell you what your reviews meant to me. The reviews posted on Amazon and Goodreads just blew me away. However, this is what they did for me.

Land was such a fun, easy write for me. It just flowed right out with a lot of laughter and a couple tears. Sea...not so much. I will honestly say that I didn't like this book. The characters were so different from the first book and there was no laughter. I knew I had to write book 2 so I could get back to Alex and her friends in book 3 but it was really hard. What made me keep going were the reviews you guys posted. Every time I wanted to trash this book, I would sit down and read what you all had to say and then keep going. That is the honest truth. Without all of your support, this book would not have been finished. I'm happy to say that around the halfway point in the book things started to change and I really got into it and started to like it. So THANK YOU!!!!!!!

This book is dedicated to all the people who took a shot on a first time writer and took the time to let me know what you thought. My husband and children who let me disappear while writing, I love you. The rest of my family and friends who cheered me on, you have my heart. To D at Book Graphics, you are an amazing artist, thank you for the covers! Okay, so…time to get to book 3 and kick a little ***!

Theresa Shaver

Contents

Chapter 1

Emily took one more look back at the gates of Disneyland before turning the corner and following her friends. She had to force herself to breathe deeply so the panic in her chest wouldn't overtake her. Choosing to go with Mason and his friends to find a boat instead of going with Alex and the others was one of the hardest choices she had ever made in her life and she still wasn't a hundred percent sure of why she had.

Emily looked around at all of the stalled and crashed cars. There were people yelling and crying all over the street. Some had bloody injuries and some were just in shock at the suddenness of the disaster. She was still trying to wrap her head around what this would mean for her future. An EMP being set off over North America was a clean way to bring America to its knees. Instead of radiation fallout and the destruction of a direct nuclear hit on land, all modern technology had fried in an instant as the burst raced through everything electrical. The lights went out, phones died, cars quit and as she had seen earlier, airplanes dropped from the sky. Being in Southern California was a very bad place to be. With no power, the water wouldn't be flowing and without transportation, food wouldn't be distributed. Couple that with a population of over ten million people in one area, and things were going to get ugly.

When Mason had told her his idea about finding a boat instead of going overland, she had thought it was a very good plan. Overland, home was fifteen hundred miles away. That seemed like a ridiculous distance to try and travel by foot or bike. A boat would let them travel all the way to Vancouver, Canada without having to physically exhaust themselves and then it was only around six hundred miles home from there. A boat was definitely the right way to go. She just desperately wished that the rest of her friends had agreed. She trusted Mason with the blindness of new love but Lisa and Mark were not high on her list of people she could rely on. When it had come time

~ 1 ~

to say goodbye to Alex she had found herself wavering. It was David's decision to accompany her that had made her decision easier. There was something about David that made her feel safe and secure when he was around. She had missed being around him in the last few months and was happy he would be traveling with them.

Mason looked back and, with a frown, waved her forward to join the group. She sped up and took his hand as they walked down the wreckage-filled street. Everyone was preoccupied with the sight of so much damage and so many hurt people. It was David that broke the silence after they had walked five blocks.

"It's going to take us all day to walk to the Marina and we'll have to make a couple stops to try and get supplies on the way. We don't want to be out walking after dark so I think we'll have to speed up as fast as we can. What do you think, Mason?" David looked to the tall quarterback. He wasn't friends with the guy but knew that he had to make an effort to work with him if they were going to make it home. David hated that Emily was dating the guy. Unfortunately, there was little choice but to trust him for now. They had a long way to go.

Mason studied David for a minute before answering him. He wasn't sure what the guy's angle was in coming with them, but Emily had raved about his resourcefulness so Mason figured he'd keep the Boy Scout close for now.

"Yeah, I think you're right, David. Who knows what this place is going to be like after the sun goes down. I really don't want to be on the streets then." He turned to Mark and Lisa, "Tighten up your laces and try to keep up you two. We need to make some serious time so we'll have to do a slow jog and then slow to speed walking when we need a break. Do you think you can do it?" he asked them.

Mark gave a nod and bent down to double tie his laces. Lisa just smirked and rolled her eyes muttering a, "Whatever."

Mason looked to Emily and David and they both nodded. When Mark stood back up, they continued down the road at a slow jog that wasn't too tiring. Every other block they came to, they would slow to a fast walk for a break. Emily concentrated on her breathing and kept her eyes on the horizon. If you kept looking up and out, it seemed to be a typical California dreamy day with blue skies and tall palm trees waving gently in the breeze. It was only at ground level that reality set in with the sight of mangled cars and injured people standing or sitting on the roads.

The lack of mechanical sound wasn't all that disturbing to Emily, having grown up in the country and not spending a great deal of time in cities. It was the human sounds filling the emptiness that bothered her. The moaning and cries of pain were the worst. Emily tried hard not to look at the injured people as she knew she couldn't help them and if she stopped for even one, they'd never make it to the Marina but that didn't stop her heart from breaking at all the pain and suffering she was passing.

They had to go around a crowd of people who were standing in the street watching a fire. A house had caught fire and it had spread to the houses on both sides of it. With no electricity, there was no water pressure and no way to fight the flames. After they had cleared the smoky area, Emily looked over her companions and was alarmed to see how red in the face Mark was. His shirt was completely drenched in sweat and his breathing was heavy. Checking the rest of the group, everyone else seemed to be holding up well. She knew Mark had a temper and tried to spare him any embarrassment by putting the focus on herself.

"Hey guys! I need a water break. Can we slow down for a few minutes, please?" she asked everyone.

Lisa stopped immediately with a moan, "Thank God! I'm a mall star, not a track star!"

She flipped her long chestnut brown hair over her shoulders and stepped further away from Mark when she noticed how sweat-drenched he was and her cat-like green eyes narrowed in disgust. The pale-skinned redhead was flushed bright red while heaving for breath between gulps from his water bottle.

Emily looked around the street corner they had stopped at and scanned the businesses across the street. Seeing a small convenience store in a strip mall, she pointed it out to the others.

"We should try and buy more water bottles and some power bars or other food from there. It seems pretty quiet right now but who knows what will happen as the day goes on."

She looked to Mason and David to see what they thought and both boys nodded their agreement so they crossed over the street and headed towards the store. There were a few cars in the parking lot but nobody in sight. The strip mall also had a computer store, luggage store and a coffee shop on one end. It was dim inside the store without the bright fluorescents on but the front windows still let in enough light to see clearly. It was also very warm without the air conditioning running. There was only one other customer in the aisles, an older lady that had a small suitcase on wheels. She paused in filling it up with canned goods to look the group of teens over, and then quickly resumed her shopping. There was a small Asian man behind the cash counter and he was scowling at them suspiciously

"You pay cash only!" he barked at them with a heavy accent.

David saw Mark's face darken in anger at the tone and quickly stepped forward to assure the store keeper. "We have cash, sir. We aren't going to be buying a lot, just some water and a little food."

The Asian man continued to glare at them but seemed mollified by David's respectful tone and he gave a brief nod toward the aisles.

They all headed towards the dark coolers at the back of the store and started to pull out water and juice bottles. They were still cool to the touch but wouldn't stay that way long with the electricity off. After adding the bottles to the plastic baskets they had gotten from the front of the store, they split up and headed down different aisles. Lisa and Emily went to the small drugstore section and grabbed items to add to their baskets. Emily did most of the shopping while Lisa was distracted by the selection of cosmetics. As she grabbed a small first aid kit and a couple bottles of pain killers, she tried to get Lisa to focus.

"We should really try and concentrate on things we will need to survive, Lisa. Makeup and nail polish won't help us," Emily said.

Lisa gave her a condescending look, "You might prefer the natural, plain look, Emily, but I have standards." She turned back to the display of makeup.

Emily was trying to think of something to say to get Lisa back on track when she heard a muffled laugh. She turned the other way and saw the older lady had joined them in the aisle and was trying to hold in her laughter. Emily smiled and headed towards her when the woman waved her closer.

In a lowered voice the older woman told her, "That cat won't change her stripes, honey. I know plenty of young missies just like her. You just go ahead and get the important stuff and let her learn." The woman looked in Emily's basket and nodded. "Don't forget the girl stuff, honey. I don't think you'll be able to run to the store once a month when you need tampons," she said with amusement when she saw Emily blush.

In a haughty voice, Lisa spoke up from behind Emily, "I won't have that problem. I'm on the Depo shot so I don't get a period."

The woman looked the smug teenage girl up and down and nodded. "You're lucky then. You won't have to worry about coming up pregnant after you've been raped a few times."

Lisa and Emily stared at the lady in complete shock. She shook her head at them like they were idiots.

"What do you think is going to happen, girlies? There will be no police driving around to the rescue and there are plenty of bad men out there that will consider this situation as a paradise. They are going to take what they want and that will be you young pretty girls. It's not a matter of if it will happen; it's a matter of when. You'd best both think on that!"

Before either girl could form a reply, the bell above the front door rang loudly as the door crashed open. All three of the women turned towards the front to see who was coming into the store. Two young men in white, wife beater tank tops and low slung baggy jeans rushed in and went straight to the front counter. The Asian man started yelling at them right away to get out but they kept going straight for him. It happened so fast. Emily couldn't believe her eyes when the taller of the men pulled a gun from behind his back and shot the shopkeeper in the head. She would have stayed standing there frozen if the older lady hadn't dragged her down. Lisa had already dropped and was starting to whimper. The older woman grabbed her by the arm and frantically motioned for her to be silent. White-faced and wide-eyed, Lisa took a deep breath and nodded. They could hear the sounds of the cash register being pried open and the sound of glass breaking. Emily was frantic with fear. She didn't know where the boys were and prayed they stayed hidden until the two men left. They were still laughing and swearing at the clerk they had just killed. The girls were towards the back of the store where the daylight had barely reached and Emily hoped that they wouldn't be seen in the dimness.

It seemed that they huddled on the floor for hours before the two men finally finished behind the counter and left the store carrying as many bottles of alcohol as they could. After a few minutes of silence, Emily heard Mason calling her name. She slowly stood on shaking legs and looked over the shelves at him. His face was white with shock.

"You and Lisa, okay?" he asked in a trembling voice.

Emily couldn't find her voice so she just nodded and turned towards the front of the store, making her way to the counter. She felt she had to check on the poor man in case he had survived. Mark was already behind the counter bent over the man. Emily assumed he was trying to find any signs of life when she saw him stand up and tuck something into the waistband of his pants. He pulled his shirt over the object and turned around.

When he saw her standing there, he flushed and abruptly said, "He's dead. Nothing we can do," and pushed past her.

Having a clear view of the body after Mark moved away, Emily could see the small bullet hole in the man's forehead. There was a spreading pool of blood under his head and she gagged at the sight. Turning quickly away from the corpse, her attention caught the small cardboard box lying beside it. There were a few small bullets in the box. Distracted by Lisa's, "So gross!" from behind her, Emily dismissed the box from her mind and moved away.

Everyone was standing at the front of the store. Mason still looked shaken and David was staring at the counter with anger. The older woman was looking the kids over and nodding her head.

"This is just the start. This city is going to burn and everyone with it. You kids better get as far away from here as you can or you'll burn with it!" she warned.

Emily nodded back at her. "We're trying. We're headed to the coast to find a boat."

"Mm hm, that's a good idea. If I was younger, I'd take a crack at that plan. You planning to lug all that stuff with you? You're going to get mighty tired carrying all that weight. You should get one of these little cases with rollers. Works real good for pulling stuff along." She paused and looked Lisa and Emily up and down. "You remember what I said, girlies. They're going to take what they want now. You best be ready for it." Looking over at the dead man, she grabbed a couple packs of cigarettes from the counter and shook her head. Without another word, she left the store.

The silence was heavy after the bell above the door stopped jangling. It was Lisa who got them moving. "The old bat is right. I don't want to be carrying all these bottles while running. I want one of those suitcases. There's a luggage store next door. Let's go get a couple," she said, looking at the boys.

Mason was nodding his head. Some color was returning to his face and he dropped his basket and headed for the door. Lisa and Mark followed him out. David turned to Emily,

"Come on, Em, let's get everything ready to pack into the cases they bring back. We need to get moving."

Emily bent down to the baskets and started to sort through all that they had grabbed. There were power bars, granola bars and beef jerky. The first aid supplies and bottled water and juices were grouped together and she couldn't help but think they wouldn't last them long. She started down the aisles and started grabbing a few more things. Cup of soup packages and instant oatmeal were light and easy to pack. Crackers and a small jar of peanut butter went in as well. The store didn't have a lot to offer as it was not a fully stocked grocery so she did her best, but knew they would need to find a better place to get supplies. There was nothing else worth carrying so she went back to the front of the store and grabbed a couple of lighters from the counter.

David was grouping supplies in piles to evenly distribute the weight when he saw Emily standing at the counter staring out the window.

"We're going to need weapons, Emily. We have to be ready to defend ourselves. That lady was right. Things are already getting bad."

She met his gaze and thought about how easily those men just shot the clerk. "David's right. We need guns," she thought. That jarred her memory and she quickly went around the counter. Trying not to look at the dead man, she reached down and picked up the small cardboard box she had seen. Taking it back to David, she handed it to him. He took out the two small bullets that were left and looked at her quizzically.

"Is there a gun back there? It would be really useful right now."

She shook her head, "I think Mark took it. I saw him stuff something down the front of his pants and cover it up with his shirt."

Davis stared at Emily intensely. "Okay, don't say anything about it. We will hope he has it but we won't push him on it. I don't know why he wouldn't say anything but I don't know why the guy would keep so quiet. We need to keep our eyes open for any other weapons we might be able to get our hands on, okay?"

Emily nodded just as the others came back into the store. They were carrying three hard-shelled, wheeled cases. Mason's and Mark's cases were plain black but Lisa's was neon pink with zebra stripes on it. Emily closed her eyes and prayed for patience. This girl was a total idiot!

"Lisa, are you trying to get yourself killed or worse? That case screams, "Look at me!" and which one of the boys will want to take a turn pulling it? Can you please start using your head here? We are very close to screwed and all you seem to care about is looking good. Grow up!" Emily was shocked at her tone as soon as the words left her mouth. She didn't mean to be so hard on the other girl but she was starting to get really scared and it had just come out.

Lisa glared daggers at Emily and threw the case down. She turned on her heel and left the store. Emily was about to go after her and apologise when Mason grabbed her hand.

"Don't. We both told her the same thing but she just ignored us. She just needs a wakeup call. If she doesn't get this new reality through her head soon, she's going to get one of us killed. Let her steam." He pulled her down and they started to fill up the two empty cases. When Lisa came back a few minutes later, she dropped a plain black case in front of them without a word and walked back down the cosmetics aisle.

It didn't take long to pack the cases up and Emily kept trying to get a look at what was in Mark's waistband but with his shirt covering it, she couldn't see anything. They left the store and started down the street again.

Chapter 2

All their breathing was strained two hours later from the smoky pall hanging in the air from the multitude of fires raging out of control in the city. They kept their pace as fast as they could but all the kids were tiring. Emily's mind was numb from the horrors they had encountered on the way. Dead and bloody bodies were littered around massive car accidents and other bodies showed signs of violence. They had to duck down and take cover at least three times. People shooting at each other and at police had pinned them down twice. The other time, a group of thugs were beating anyone they could find and Emily felt like her heart would explode out of her chest at the senseless violence on display. She couldn't understand how things had gotten so bad so fast. They weren't the only people pulling luggage on the streets as others tried to make their escape from the battlefield the city had now become. The strangest sights were of people rushing out of stores carrying flat screen TV's or computers. Didn't these people understand that those items had no value without electricity? Once they had made it onto the Garden Grove Freeway, the landscape had changed from residential to business and that was where the shooting had started. Gunfire could be heard constantly, and Emily was starting to doubt that they would make it to the coast. They still had so far to go and needed to find supplies.

David and Mason had studied the map that Cooper had gotten before they left Disneyland but they needed to find one of their own. Things were degrading fast and they needed to be able to find alternate routes. They had slowed down to catch their breath when they came upon a small privately owned gas station that had no looters in the parking lot. Three big men that resembled each other were standing guard in front of the pumps. Each man was holding a shotgun pointed towards the street to dissuade any looters from coming closer. The kids stopped at the edge of the lot and had a quick conference. They needed a map and the gas station should have one. Mason was more than happy to let David approach the gun-toting men. David turned away from the group and put his hands in the air, slowly walking towards the men. When all three shotgun barrels swung in his direction, his stomach lurched but he took a few more steps before stopping.

"Please don't shoot, sir! I have money and was just hoping to buy a map. My friends and I are just trying to find a way out of the city but we're tourists and don't know the area." David took a shaky breath while the men looked him over. The men looked like family to David and it was the older man who finally gave a brief nod. He lowered the business end of his gun toward the pavement but kept it pointing in David's general direction. The other two men both turned back to focus on the street. The older man waved David forward and started backing towards the store entrance.

"I've got a rack just inside the door, full of maps. Where you kids trying to get to?" he asked David in a gruff voice.

"Canada, Alberta, sir."

The man's eyebrows shot up in surprise and his face softened slightly. "Me and my boys went and did some hunting in northern British Columbia two years ago. Beautiful country up there and the nicest people. That's an awful long ways away. How are you planning on getting up there?"

David was thankful the man had relaxed his grip on the weapon and seemed friendlier. "We're hoping to make it to the coast and try and find a ride by boat further north."

The man was thoughtful for a moment before nodding. "Not a bad plan. If you could get clear of the major cities, you'd have a better chance overland." He opened the door of the store and waved David ahead of him. The spinning rack just inside the door held all types of road maps and the man gave it a spin until he found what he wanted. "This one here is a local street map. It'll help you find your way to the marina." He spun the rack again and grabbed three thicker map books. "This one's

California and here's Oregon and this one's Washington. That way, wherever you land, you'll know which way to go. Sorry I don't have anything for Canada but these will help," he said while handing the bunch over.

David started to reach in to his pocket but froze when the man brought his gun back up with a frown.

"Money, sir! I'm just getting my money!"

The gun dipped back down and the man shook his head. "No need, son. Money doesn't mean anything now. Just take them and get going. You kids have a long way to go. Good luck."

He ushered David back out of the store and waved him on towards his friends who were grouped at the edge of the lot looking anxious. Halfway back to them, David stopped and turned back. He gave a wave and called out, "Thank you, good luck!" The three men all gave a nod and went back to scanning the street for threats.

When he got to his friends, Emily let out a sigh of relief and took the three map books he held out to put them in one of the cases. David opened the local map and he and Mason scanned around the area to find a street sign. Emily noticed Mark glaring at David when he and Mason studied the map together and hoped he wouldn't start any trouble. When they found what they were looking for, they pored over the map and plotted out the route they needed. Satisfied they knew where they were and where they needed to go, David folded the map back up and put it into the side cargo pocket of his shorts.

Mason addressed the rest of the group, "Okay, we still have a long way to go. We'll stay on this road for a few hours until we turn onto a road named Seal Beach Boulevard and Marine Drive. After that, it's straight to the marina and hopefully some waves. Keep your eyes open for trouble." He grabbed the handle of a rolling case and started away from them. Mark and David grabbed their cases and headed after him with Mark elbowing David out of the way so he could get ahead of him. Emily and Lisa trailed behind. Lisa heaved out a dramatic sigh.

"This is so not my idea of a California vacation. As if we have to walk for hours more! This is so lame. God, I would kill for a Frappuccino!" she complained in a dramatic tone with a huge eye roll.

Emily couldn't believe how vapid the girl was. She knew that Lisa was shallow and spoiled but she didn't seem to get the situation they were in at all. Emily hoped that Lisa would clue in soon or she wasn't going to be any help to the rest of them. Emily tried to be understanding but she was scared and babying Lisa wasn't going to help any.

"Lisa, you get what's happened right? We aren't just going to be walking for hours more. It's going to take us a really long time to get home, like a month or more. Even if we get out of here on a boat and make it to Vancouver, we still have to cross B.C. and get over the mountains. We'll be walking for weeks. This is really bad," Emily tried to explain.

With another eye roll and a smirk, her voice virtually dripping with disdain, she replied, "I know all of you seem to think this is the apocalypse and all but really, really? The government will get it sorted out. There's too much money in this country for it to stay messed up for long. I'm sure we'll be fine as soon as we get out of this hellhole of a city. You'll see. We'll be home in no time," she finished with confidence.

Emily shook her head. "I hope you're right, Lisa, but until we get out of here, let's work together, okay?"

Lisa gave her a fake, tight little smile and a quick nod then quickened her pace until she was walking beside Mason. Emily practiced an eye roll of her own at the girl's back and huffed out a sigh. "Where's Alex when I need her," she thought. Looking around at the businesses they were passing, Emily noticed a lot of signs with Asian lettering and many had steel security doors blocking off their doors and windows. This city was so foreign to her. She had grown up in the country and Prairie Springs, the town closest to her farm, wasn't even close to being a city. All these people on the streets made her nervous and she was anxious to be far away. She picked up her pace and closed the gap with the rest of the group.

The street they were traveling on seemed to go on forever and the kids started to become numb to the bodies on the street and in cars that they passed. The gunshots had become less frequent and they hadn't seen any violence in the last few hours. Their pace had slowed down and none of them had the energy to jog anymore. Mason, who was leading the group, came to a stop and turned to David.

Waving behind him, he asked, "What do you think?"

David studied the huge warehouse type store and the people who were pushing loaded carts out of it. "I think we should give it a shot. If we can get a couple of carts full of supplies it would go a long way to bribing someone to give us a ride out of here. Not many Costco stores on the ocean."

"Yeah, we can carry a lot more weight if it is piled up in the shopping carts. Everyone look around and try and find a cart." Mason said as he started scanning the lot.

The parking area was only half-filled with dead cars and the group looked down the rows trying to find any abandoned carts. They finally found one wedged between two cars and they all headed into the huge store. There was an open foyer at the front of the store between the two sets of doors and Emily was happy to see one row of carts left along the wall. They decide that three carts were enough so Emily pulled one out and so did David.

In the main warehouse of the store, someone had set up battery powered construction lights, and with the skylights, it was good enough to see by. It was still dim and warm but they were able to navigate around other people and goods that had been spilled onto the floor. After passing the now useless electronics section, they had to go around piles of smashed glass from the jewellery cases. After that, they hit the aisles of snack goods. Bags of nuts and trail mix were thrown into the carts and cases of power bars, big bags of beef jerky and big boxes of granola bars were also added. They passed by the linens section and came to tables piled with clothing. All of their clothing was back in the hotel that the class had been staying in so they started rummaging through the piles to find extra outfits. Emily was thankful that there were piles of yoga wear and quickly found her sizes. She grabbed a bag of socks and under wear and found a table that had light fleece jackets. Ready to move on to the next aisle she wasn't surprised to find Lisa hadn't gotten past the first table. The girl was holding clothes up to her body to make sure it looked good.

It took Emily two seconds to decide to leave her to it. She wanted to get out of here and back on the way as fast as she could. Grabbing her cart, she pushed it away from the clothing area. The boys had finished up in clothing as fast as she had and split up. She could just make out Mason and Mark heading deeper into the store. David had gone the opposite direction and he disappeared down an aisle with batteries. On her own, Emily started on the bulk food. Cases of tuna, canned ham, chilli and beans took up space in the cart. Huge bags of rice and just add water pancake mix were heaved in. Emily didn't want to take too much canned food because of the weight so she added bags of dried vegetables and fruit. The store had huge boxes full of ramen noodles but it was too awkward to take in her cart so she opened the case and started stuffing the individually wrapped squares in around the other cases and bags in her cart. Boxes of crackers and cookies went in and a box of instant oatmeal packages barely fit as well. Ahead of her was the freezers so she by passed them and continued on. Without thinking it through, she grabbed a huge can of ground coffee but it only took a few steps before she stopped with a shake of her head. Putting the can back she instead took three jars of instant. Her cart was piled high as she added four bags of dried milk powder. The rest of the store held fresh food and bottled water. She didn't have enough room left for the water so she headed to the pharmacy area. Big bottles of multivitamins and Vitamin C were squeezed in as well as a much bigger first aid kit.

As Emily turned down the next aisle, she saw Lisa scanning the shampoos. Lisa had a few items of clothing draped over her arm and a handful of fashion magazines held against her chest. She looked over and spotted Emily coming her way and scowled at her.

"Finally! You left me to haul this stuff around when you took off with the cart," she said impatiently.

"Hey, thanks so much for your help, Lisa, but don't worry I'm sure I got enough to feed you too!" Emily replied sarcastically.

An eye roll and a "Whatever!" was all she had to say as she dumped her stuff on top of the overflowing cart. "Make some room in there. I need to fit in this shampoo and conditioner," she demanded.

Emily was fuming and had to get away from Lisa before she said something vicious so she just pushed past her. "You'll have to carry it yourself. There is no room."

Lisa whined at Emily's back, "But it's heavy!"

"So is this cart!" was all Emily tossed back at her. She could hear Lisa growling in frustration and couldn't help but rub it in by grabbing a men and women's five pack of deodorant and shoving it into the cart. When she heard Lisa squeal in outrage she had to smile and pushed it even more by pulling a large bottle of hand sanitizer off the shelf as well. Leaving the pharmacy area, Emily couldn't remember anyone pushing her to act so petty and shook her head at the childish behaviour. This trip home was going to be hell.

She spotted David pushing his cart her way with Mason and Mark close behind. Both of their carts were stacked with water bottle cases and clothes. David's cart had two multi packs of flashlights and packages of batteries. He also had five sturdy back packs. Emily was happy she had just stuck with getting the food or they would all starve.

The three carts came together and they all started to distribute the food and water to make the weight loads more even. When Mason held up the fashion magazines,

Emily just shook her head and mumbled Lisa's name so he stuffed them in where he could.

David happened to look up and with a frown moved away from the carts. They all turned to see where he was going and saw him meet up with Lisa. He was taking bottles out of her arms and when she saw Emily watching she poured on the charm.

"Thank you so much, David! You are so sweet. I tried to grab as much as I could for us but without a cart this is all I could manage," she gushed and flirted with him.

David looked at the bottles and tried to smile. "Ok, thanks for the sunscreen and toothbrushes and paste. That's a good idea but I don't think the hair conditioner will be of much use." He gave her a quick smile and turned away.

Emily had to turn away as well, or she would end up laughing at Lisa. She caught sight of Mason's stormy face and hoped he wouldn't be too hard on Lisa. They all had a long way to go and there was already enough friction in the group. She was completely surprised when Mason snatched the bottles out of David's hands and shoved the cart past him, pushing him to the side. Why would Mason be mad at David? She was even more confused at the nasty smirk on Mark's face as he pushed past with David's cart. Staring at the back of Mason's head as he whispered to Lisa, Emily had a brief flash that Mason was upset about Lisa's flirting with David. Shaking her head at the thought, she dismissed it. He was just being a jerk.

"Let me push that, Em." David said and she moved away from the cart so he could get behind it.

They pushed their carts through the empty checkout stands and Emily had to look away from the two dead bodies with name tags pinned to their chests. They had both been shot and their bodies lay in pools of blood. Emily felt her stomach heave a little when she saw the shopping cart wheel tracks that had left a trail of blood all the way out the door. She was already getting desensitized from all the death she had seen, but the evidence of people pushing their carts past the dead men and through their blood was appalling to her. Emerging out of the dim store into the bright afternoon sun was welcome and she took a deep breath only to start coughing from the smoky air. She couldn't wait to get away from this city.

They made their way back through the parking lot and started down the street again. The EMP had been set off hours ago and the streets had emptied of people. There were still people walking but most of the wrecked cars sat empty. As the day progressed, most people had realized that emergency services weren't coming and they had walked away from the accidents and headed to hospitals or homes. They had only been pushing the heavy carts for a half an hour when Lisa started to complain about her feet. She wanted to stop for a while and rest. Everyone was tired and ignored her. Emily's feet were throbbing but she knew they had to get to the marina before night or they might not make it out alive.

A few men eyed the loaded carts but Mark and Mason stared them down and they passed by without incident. Emily knew that they would end up in a confrontation at some point and was scared. They hadn't found any weapons and she hoped their luck would hold out.

With no one listening to her, Lisa had stopped her whining and was trudging along with the rest of them until they came to a huge green space. Her head came up and she looked through the chain link fence at the beautifully manicured lawn. "Look, it's a park! We can stop and rest for a while and have something to eat. Please guys? I just want to sit down for a while," she pleaded.

Mason looked over at the park and shook his head. "It's not a park, it's a golf course. The fence will go all the way around it. We can't get in and if we stop and sit, your feet will hurt even more when you get back up. Come on, Lisa, it's only a few more hours. Suck it up!"

Lisa moaned in pain and frustration, "I would love to be sitting in a golf cart right now," she moaned.

They had only gone ten feet when David came to an abrupt stop. "Wait!" he turned to Lisa, "What did you say?"

She looked at him in hope. "We can stop and sit in the grass for a break!"

"No. The last thing you said, sitting in a golf cart." He turned to Mason who was looking impatient. "Golf carts. They should still work, no fancy electronics. We can get a couple and drive them the rest of the way."

Mason shook his head, "Nice thought, but they would all be the fancy kind, full of electronics. The newer carts even have GPS."

David grinned, "Yeah, but I bet the maintenance carts are the older ones and they would have storage spaces on the back to haul groundskeeper tools. We should check. It could save us a couple of hours."

Mason was thinking about it with a thoughtful expression but Mark was sick of the Boy Scout so he butted in. "Let's go already. We would just be wasting time looking for them," he said forcefully.

David nodded, "Yeah, okay but just let me climb this fence to the top. If I see anything we can try for them, otherwise we'll keep going." Without waiting for a reply, David quickly scaled the fence and stood on the top scanning the course. It only took him minutes to drop back down and everyone looked at him expectantly. "I can see the roof of a building in the direction we're heading but I don't know what it is so let's keep going and I'll climb up again when we get further."

They continued on down the street for another ten minutes before David climbed the fence again. He dropped back quickly and shook his head so they kept going. Lisa was letting out little whimpers and Emily tried hard to ignore her as her own feet throbbed in sympathy. The lush green lawns seemed to go on forever before Emily could see a cross street coming up and the end of the golf course. As they neared the end of the fence, they could all see a small building with a garage door. They stopped the shopping carts beside the fence and David climbed over and dropped to the other side of it. He disappeared around the side of the building out of sight.

"What a waste of time. Who's this guy think he is, MacGyver?" Mark growled.

Before anyone could respond, David came back around with a grin on his face. "There's a window on the other side. I could see four of the old style carts in there and they all have truck bed style areas on the back so we can load the supplies."

"How are we going to get them out?" Mason asked, still not convinced.

"We break the window and get the door up. There are all kinds of tools inside we can use. Then we cut the fence and peel it back and drive them right out."

Mark started to laugh, "Some Boy Scout you are, break and entering, stealing private property and damaging property. What's next, Dave? You want to go rob a liquor store? I might just start to like you after all!"

David frowned at the big red head. "It's too late to be worrying about stealing now," as he waved at the loaded carts. "And it's not like we're hurting anyone. This could help save our lives so I'm okay with it. It might be wrong but desperate times and all. You going to help me with this or what?" he asked.

"I'm your man! Stand back." Mark scaled the fence and with a grunt heaved himself over.

Chapter 3

Emily held the fence back as Mason drove the last of the three golf carts they were taking through and onto the sidewalk. They emptied all the shopping carts into the back storage areas and climbed in. Lisa didn't help with the loading but dropped into the seat of the first one out and didn't budge. There were only two seats per cart so they had to take three and Mark was happy to drive his alone. Emily rode with Mason and David was stuck with Lisa. When Lisa offered David a smile and a power bar, Emily thought she could see a tightening of Mason's face but she ignored it. They were all stressed and David wasn't a part of Mason's social group but she hoped he would warm up to him.

Her feet were screaming in relief from finally being able to sit down after being on them for hours. She didn't have a watch but from the position of the sun, she knew it was late afternoon. As the golf cart jerked forward, she turned around and pulled out two water bottles and some beef jerky for her and Mason. They had barely spoken all day and this was the first time that they had been alone. Emily snuggled closer to him and he gave her a quick kiss on the head before turning back to drive. The extra wide sidewalks had no problem accommodating the narrow golf carts and they didn't have to worry about the smashed up vehicles blocking the road. They weren't traveling as fast as a car would but it was way faster than walking.

Groups of people watched them as they went by but only one woman tried to flag them down. Emily looked away as they passed her and she was suddenly saddened by not stopping to help anyone all day. The street they had been following turned into a true freeway and they had to navigate around more crashes as the sidewalks ended. It slowed them down and at one point the boys had to push a couple cars out of the way that had completely blocked the road forward. The only people left on the freeway were the ones that were too injured to walk away and Emily knew that those poor people were doomed. No one was coming to help. More than once, she felt tears streaming down her face and Mason would squeeze her leg in comfort but they always drove on. She felt a huge amount of guilt and couldn't help but think of her family, wondering if they were also injured as people walked past them without helping. She tried to think about where her parents would have been when the pulse stopped everything. Her mom worked in town but she didn't leave for work until eight, so with the time difference she would have still been at home, not driving. Her dad worked on the farm so he would have been there as well. She was an only child so she didn't have any siblings. Alex was as close as a sister would be and Emily felt guilt again at leaving her. She worried about Alex and her other friends that had gone overland and hoped that they were safe and were making good time getting out of the city.

Emily guessed that it had to be around five o'clock when they started to see overhead signs announcing their exit. She was thankful for the wide lane streets that made it easy to go around crashes. They had only made it a few blocks on Seal Beach Blvd when Mark, who was in the lead, came to a quick stop. Mason was about to get out and see what had made him stop when they heard the loud sounds of engines. Within seconds, a convoy of military vehicles passed through the intersection that they had stopped at. There were six all together and one had a gunner on top with the biggest gun Emily had ever seen pointed in their direction. Lisa was bouncing up and down in her seat waving at the men who stared out at them grim-faced. Only the gunner acknowledged her with a brief nod and then they were gone. Before anyone could get out and talk about what they had just seen, Mark started forward through the intersection and they were forced to follow.

They started passing businesses and as they passed a Starbucks, Emily could see Lisa pointing and talking to David. "She's probably trying to get him to go through the drive thru for a Frappuccino," Emily thought to herself. She sighed and told herself to stop being catty. She was going to have to have more patience with Lisa if the rest of the trip was to be manageable. Constantly sniping at each other would only make things more difficult. If she wanted Mason and Mark to treat David better, she would have to do the same with Lisa. She turned slightly in her seat and studied Mason.

He was so good looking that it still sent a thrill through her knowing he was her boyfriend. His streaked hair gleamed in the sun and a slight frown didn't take away from his handsome face. Emily smiled slightly at the memory of how much she disliked him when she first started to tutor him. Initially, he was egotistical and arrogant but the longer they worked together, the more she saw a different side to him. When he realized she wasn't impressed by him, he started to treat her better. Talking on the phone about school work changed into talking about other things in their lives. He told her about his family and how much pressure his dad put on him to be the best in football. He was living under his older brother's huge shadow. His brother, Brett, had been an all-star in high school and had won a full scholarship to university where he was the starting quarterback for his team. Mason's dad expected the same thing from him and he struggled to live up to it.

When he had finally asked her out, it was with humility and she fell for him. Mason's friends, however, were a different story. Mark mainly ignored her but Lisa was nasty from the start. She would make catty little comments when Mason wasn't there to hear them and then pretend to be nice in front of him. Emily tried hard to get along with them but it was a struggle. She didn't like the way Mark would bully other people or the way Lisa seemed to look down on anyone she felt was inferior. When Alex started to give her a hard time about dating Mason, she couldn't handle it and had started distancing herself from her best friend, spending more and more time with Mason's group. She really regretted that now and wished fiercely for Alex to be with them.

She decided to talk to Mason about David and try and get him to be nicer to her friend. "This is so much better than walking. I'm glad David came with us, aren't you?" she asked.

"Yeah, he's a total hero," he replied sarcastically.

"Mason! What's wrong with David? He's a really nice guy and all he's done is help out so far. Why don't you like him?"

He huffed out a breath, "You're right. I'm sorry. He has been a great help. I just don't know what his angle is. At first I thought he was interested in you but now I think he's into Lisa."

Emily laughed, "David has been one of my best friends since I was eight years old. Don't you think if he was interested in me he would have made his move before now? And Lisa is so not his type but so what if he is into her. Maybe he'll rub off on her and she will start being a decent human being. As for his angle, you could try the truth. He has a mom and little sister all alone at home and he wants to get back to them as fast as possible. He's worried about them and thought the boat would get him home quicker. Why do you think everyone has some hidden agenda...do you?"

"No, I just don't know him, that's all. You're right, Em, we're lucky he came with us," he conceded and gave her leg a squeeze.

She rested her head against his shoulder, happy he had come around. She was so tired from the physical and emotional day that she felt herself nodding off. Catching herself, she sat up straighter and asked Mason, "Do you think you can get a boat out of the marina? Are they that easy to steal? Do you think we should try and find someone to give us a ride first?" she asked, trying to stay alert.

Mason laughed and said, "Whoa there, you sound like your motor mouth friend, Alex," which earned him a punch in the arm.

"Okay, okay sorry, but she does talk fast and fires off questions like that. We shouldn't have any problem finding an older boat with an engine that works but to tell you the truth I would feel better getting a ride with

~ 25 ~

someone more experienced. I've sailed on lakes but never in the open ocean and I'm a little nervous about tackling that on my own. Hopefully, we'll find someone who is heading north and we can bribe them with the food and water we have. Won't know until we get there though."

Emily appreciated that Mason was honest with her about his fears. She knew he never would have admitted it in front of the others. She looked ahead and saw Mark was slowing down at an intersection. The sign read Marina Dr. They were getting closer and she started thinking about what they could do if they couldn't find anyone to give them a ride.

"If we can't find anyone to help us, what do you think about finding something small with a motor? We could at least get clear of the major cities by staying close to shore," she asked him.

"Yeah, I thought about that. We wouldn't get very far but at least we wouldn't be walking through that hellhole. We'll keep it in mind as a last ditch effort."

Emily was about to ask another question when gunshots rang out loud and close by. She saw Mark swerve his cart to one side of the street behind a car. He scrambled out and ducked down. David was just as fast, stopping behind a delivery truck and Emily saw him yank Lisa out and down onto the pavement. Mason slammed their golf cart to a stop in the middle of the street and frantically scanned around to find out where the shooting was coming from. The glass windshield of a car parked beside them suddenly exploded and with a scream, Emily dove out and crawled to the back of the cart. Mason was still sitting behind the steering wheel and didn't even seem to hear Emily screaming at him to get down.

Emily peeked around the back of the cart to see what was happening and screamed at Mason again. She was leaning against the back bumper when it suddenly lurched forward and sped away, leaving her exposed in the middle of the street. A sob of terror burst out of her as she scrabbled to the nearest car for cover on her hands and knees. She was panting hard by the time she made it and her heart felt like it would burst out of her chest. Whimpering in fear, she eased over to see around the car. Mark and David's carts were still there on the side of the road but Mason's was getting further and further away. Movement to the left caught her eye and she turned her head to see two uniformed police officers rush into the street from between two buildings. They crouched down and moved from cover to cover. A gunshot rang out from the still unseen assailant and the two cops immediately returned fire. Emily must have screamed because one of the cops turned his weapon at her. With a scowl, he faced away again and scanned the area. His partner pointed further down and across the street and moved forward. The cop who had seen Emily made to follow but stopped and turned back to her.

"Wait for two and then go!" he hissed at her.

With her hands covering her mouth to hold back another scream, she just nodded as the cop moved away. Emily's whole body was shaking with fear and shock. Mason had left her. That he had left her to die was all she could think of as her eyes tracked the police officers down the road until they were out of sight. She waited another minute and then still crouching ran towards David and Lisa. When she bumped into the back of their golf cart, Lisa made a sharp squeal of fright and whipped her head around. Lisa's eyes were as big as saucers and shimmered with tears. When she saw it was Emily, she launched herself at her and clung tight.

Emily met David's eyes over the sobbing girl's shoulder and mouthed, "Let's go!"

He nodded and pried Lisa away from Emily. The three squeezed into the golf cart and David started to roll it forward. When they got even with the other cart, David stage-whispered, "Mark, let's go!" and continued on. Emily looked back to make sure Mark was coming and turned forward when she saw him jump behind the wheel. David glanced back and when he saw the other cart following, he sped up. Lisa and Emily jolted at the sound of another gunshot but it was further away from them this time. Lisa was clutching Emily's arm painfully while she sobbed and shook. Even though Emily was terrified as well, she freed her arm and wrapped it around Lisa and tried to comfort her.

Once they had cleared the area, David slowed down and turned to look at Emily, his face a mix of bewilderment and rage.

"What the hell, Emily! What happened back there? Did Mason ditch you?!"

Emily couldn't speak yet, she was still shocked stupid by Mason's actions so she just lowered her head against Lisa's and closed her eyes.

Chapter 4

The sun was slowly making its way to the horizon as they continued down Marine Drive. Lisa had stopped sobbing but she stayed pressed against Emily and she hadn't spoken since the shooting. Even though they had never been friends, Emily was comforted by the girl's closeness. Her mind couldn't seem to settle down. Mason had left her exposed in the middle of the street and had driven away without a backwards glance. Everything she thought she knew about him was in doubt. How could he have done that to her and what did that mean for the rest of the journey home? She bit her lip to keep the sob back when she thought of choosing him over Alex and the rest of her friends. A sound from David brought her head up and she looked ahead down the street. She could see the top of masts in the distance as the marina got closer. Lowering her sight to the street, she could see a bridge that led to the marina area and parked to one side of it was Mason in his golf cart. He was still behind the wheel but his head was in his hands.

As they got closer to him, he heard the engines and his head whipped up to stare at them. David stopped the cart half a block away and Mark zipped around them and drove straight to Mason, pulling up beside him. When Lisa realized they had stopped, she sat up and looked around. When she saw Mason, she made a little whimper and scrambled over Emily and out of the cart, running the rest of the way to him.

David and Emily didn't speak for a minute. They just sat and stared at the group ahead of them. Without looking at her, David reached over and took Emily's hand, giving it a squeeze.

"We could just go. You and me, we could leave them here and find our own boat. Something small with a motor. We could stay close to shore and get past the city and then head overland. I would get you home, Emily. I would protect you."

Emily studied Mason and his friends. "I don't belong with them. David's right, we'd be better off without them. We can't count on them at all," she thought. Just as she was about to tell David yes, Mason broke away from the others and ran towards them.

"Emily, are you okay?! I'm so sorry! I don't know what happened. I just froze. My mind was screaming go go go and I just panicked. Please believe me! I'm so sorry. Please forgive me!" he pleaded.

Emily could see tears in his eyes and his face was full of shame and guilt. She remembered how he had just sat there with bullets flying and realized that what he said was probably true but how could she ever trust him again? Once again she was going to tell David that they would go when Mason said something that changed her mind.

"Emily…I love you."

David groaned and Mason shot him a dirty look before swinging his eyes back to Emily.

"Please. It won't happen again. You can count on me." His eyes were full of sincerity.

Emily found herself nodding and she looked to David. "We should stay together, right?" she asked him with confusion. David let out a long sigh.

"I'm with you, no matter what you decide," he told her, looking miserable.

Hesitantly, she nodded again. "Okay…we'll just keep going together…Okay?"

"Yeah, alright, let's go find a boat and get out of here," David replied, turning and looking straight ahead.

Mason leaned in and squeezed Emily's arm and nodded. Then he turned and jogged back to the others. As David drove them over the bridge, Emily thought about what Mason had said. She was still shaken and upset with what he had done, but she could understand why it had happened. None of them were mentally prepared for what had happened today and they were all going to make mistakes. She was shocked that he had said, "I love you". They had been dating for a few months and she really liked him but love was the big scary. It was something she would have to think about.

David pulled up to the marina parking area and waited. His face was grim as he watched Mason and Mark drive farther into the lot. How could Emily be so blind? The guy was a selfish coward. He had left her on that street to die and then played the love card? And she fell for it? He was beginning to think he should have just gone with the others. He wanted to help Emily but she had to start thinking or they would end up in serious trouble.

David drove the golf cart deeper into the marina to where the others had stopped. There was a clubhouse and restaurants with a parking lot ahead of them and then docks filled with all types of sailing craft. David was surprised to not see any people. He had figured there would be some people with the same idea as them about getting out of the city. As he scanned the boat slips, he started to see that there were many open spaces. It was late in the day so David guessed that a lot of people had already made it to the marina and left by boat. He just hoped that they could find someone still here that would give them a ride. The thought of Mason in control of one of these huge boats filled him with fear. Panicking on the street was bad enough but if he froze out in the middle of the ocean, they would all die.

They pulled all three carts up to the walkway to the docks and shut the engines down. Mark ran over to the clubhouse and checked the doors but they were locked up tight. They all stood at the walkway scanning boats and then turned to look at Mason expectantly. When he just stood looking out at the boats, David shook his head impatiently.

"So what are we looking for Mason? Should we just start walking down docks looking for any one onboard?"

Mason didn't look at him. Now that they had made it here, he was intimidated by all the different sailing craft that he only had basic knowledge of. His confidence had been rocked by how he had reacted on the street and he was afraid of losing even more face by making another wrong decision. He glanced at Mark and Lisa and tried to catch Emily's eye but she wouldn't look at him. Swallowing past the knot of uncertainty in his throat, he turned to David.

"Yeah, let's just walk up and down the docks and see if anyone is around." He started down the walkway when David spoke up.

"Someone has to stay with the carts. We can't lose the supplies."

"I'll stay. I don't know anything about boats anyway. Just hurry up and find us a ride. The sun's going to be down soon and I don't want to be here when the crazies come out to play," Mark volunteered.

"Okay, thanks, man," David said and pushed past Mason onto the dock and jogged down to the end.

There were lots of huge cruising yachts but no sailboats. David guessed that the fancy yachts would be just as dead as all the cars on the road with all their electronics fried. He turned back and headed for the next dock. They continued down each dock this way with no luck until they had reached the twelfth one and David heard banging and a muffled curse. Halfway down the dock he came to a stop at a forty or fifty foot sailboat. It was in between two cruisers and David could see piles of supplies and bags sitting on its deck. All the other boats had empty decks so David was sure someone was onboard. When he heard the bang come again, he closed his eyes in relief, finally, a chance to get help. He turned and waved Mason and the girls forward and pointed at the huge sail boat.

When they had all caught up to him, he said, "I'm going to call out to whoever's on it. I'm going to be very polite and respectful. We need to try and convince this person to help us so everyone needs to put their best face forward. No attitude and no eye rolling," pointedly looking at Mason and Lisa.

For once Lisa parked her attitude and nodded solemnly. She still hadn't recovered from the close call on the street and was willing to do anything to get out of the city and away to safety. Mason was a different story. He immediately scowled at David and took a step towards him.

"Who put you in charge, Boy Scout?" He almost spat.

David stared him down and through gritted teeth told him, "Someone's got to get us out of here and we all learned that running away isn't going to work so just shut up and lose the ego and work with me here."

Mason took another menacing step forward but before he could cut into David, Emily put her hand on his chest and pushed him back.

"That's enough, Mason! I want out of here and David's right. We have to sell this person on helping us so just be nice for once." Mason looked at her with a hurt expression but finally stepped back and nodded at David.

David turned to the boat and called out, "Hello, on the boat! Anyone aboard?" There were a few moments of silence before they heard the sound of a door shutting and steps on the stairs. A man's head came into view as he came on deck and stared down at them. He was tall with a dark tan. He was wearing tan cargo shorts and a tee-shirt that showed strong arms and hands that were covered in grease. He took in the group of kids with a neutral expression on his face. When he didn't say anything, David stepped forward.

"Hi, we heard you banging around and we just wondered if you had heard any news about what's going on?" David didn't want to just hit the guy with, "Can you take us home?" He wanted to get him talking and build a rapport with him.

The man pulled a rag out of his back pocket and started to clean the grease off his hands before answering, "Not really, but it's bad, really bad. Nothing electronic is working and the city is breaking down fast. Fires and gunshots everywhere. It took me all day to get here on foot," he replied with a grimace.

David nodded. "Yeah, we saw some bad stuff too. We were at Disneyland on a class trip when everything stopped. Saw a plane drop out of the sky and on the way here, there were bodies all over the place. Our teacher thinks it was an EMP."

"An EMP…that would explain a lot." The man looked around and back down the dock before focusing back on David. "Where's your teacher?"

"Not with us. She told us to try and get out of the city. Some of the other kids headed inland but we wanted to try taking a boat out. Mrs. Moore stayed back with the kids that wouldn't leave. They think the government will come and rescue them so they're headed to the consulate."

The man scoffed, "They won't make it. No one's coming and if they did, there are millions of people here to help. What consulate, where are you guys from?"

"Canada, Alberta. We're going to try and get a boat working and head up the coast to B.C. and head overland from there."

"Man, I love Alberta. I've done a lot of skiing around Banff. I'm originally from the Seattle area so it's a quick hop up there. At least it was." He paused thoughtfully with a frown. "Do you guys even know how to sail? Nothing that's engine-powered will work, at least nothing newer. You might be able to find an old tub that you could get working but you'd never get enough fuel to get that far."

Mason, who had been standing back stepped forward and tried to sound confident. "I've done some sailing on small boats but only on lakes, never in the ocean. I thought we would stay close to shore and get as far north as we could."

The man was shaking his head halfway through Mason's plan. "That won't work. If you don't have experience with the tides and currents you would be wrecked in no time. That stretch is the last place you want to learn. It's better to head out towards Hawaii and then turn northeast. Trust me, I've made the trip twice a year for the past 6 years. You guys would be better off finding something powered."

Everyone visibly slumped in defeat. Everything in this marina looked newer which meant fried electronics.

The man frowned again. "Do any of you guys know anything about engines?"

David's head came up, "Yes, sir, I've been working on them for as long as I can remember."

The man looked the kids over again. "So you know about engines and you know a little about sailing." He shook his head. "Just enough to get into trouble or get very lucky. What about supplies? You can't just go to the store while you're out on the water and it would be weeks to go that far."

Emily decided to make their case. The sun was getting even lower and she wanted to move on if this guy wasn't going to help them so she spoke up. "We have three golf carts over there filled with food and water. We have enough with rationing to last that long. Water will be the biggest worry but we can hope for rain." She stopped and took a breath. "Sir, David is really amazing with engines and Mason has some sailing experience. We have a lot of supplies and can take care of ourselves. If we stay here, we will die or worse. It's too late for us to try and walk out of the city now. We have to go by boat as far as we can get. Will you help us? Will you take us with you?"

The man took a step back in surprise as if he hadn't even considered it. Before he could respond, she introduced everyone. "I'm Emily and this is Lisa. The boys are David and Mason. Our friend Mark is guarding the supplies over there. Twenty minutes ago we were shot at and almost killed. If Lisa and I are caught by the wrong people, we'll be raped and then killed. I'm only sixteen. I don't want to die. We have to get out of here and soon." She looked at the man pleadingly.

"I...I don't...Oh, man!" he stuttered.

David jumped in again. "We'd do anything you want. We can help in anyway and we'd stay out of your way. You can share all the supplies we brought and we can scavenge more from around here. We can get more gas from these boats and find more water. We'd do anything! Please, sir, help us get home."

The man looked up into the sky and then rubbed his hands over his face. "Argg! Okay, but I can't take you to B.C. I'm only going as far as Washington. You'll have to find your own way from there!"

Emily sobbed out a 'thank you' and turned to Lisa and hugged her. She was so happy that they were getting out of here that she didn't even care when the girl pushed her away. Mason and David were thanking the man who introduced himself as Tim Greyson.

"Alright, we only have about an hour before we lose the light to navigate out of here. We should really just stay here for tonight but I'm worried about looters and gangs showing up, not to mention the fires that are burning out of control. So go get your friend. You should be able to just drive the golf carts right out onto the dock. We'll load up and see about getting some more gas. Most of the boats will have jerrycans on board and extra water. We'll grab whatever we can in the next forty minutes and then we're out of here."

While Mason and David jogged back to get the golf carts and Mark, Emily and Lisa boarded the boat.

"Ladies, welcome to the Lawless," Tim said.

Lisa just laughed at the name but Emily froze and turned concerned eyes to him.

When he saw her apprehension, Tim was quick to explain. "No, no, it's not like that! I'm a lawyer and sailing is my escape from work, hence the name. Don't worry - you guys are safe with me. I've got two younger sisters that I adore and the thought of them being stuck in this city was one of the main reasons I agreed to take you guys with me."

Emily's expression softened and she smiled gratefully at him. "You really are saving our lives. We probably wouldn't have made it two days in there," she said as she waved towards the smoky cityline.

"Hey, Tim, do you have a washroom on board? It would be great if we could get cleaned up. We've been walking all day," Lisa asked with a flirty smile.

"Oh, yeah, sure I'll give you a quick tour while we wait for your friends to get back. Come on down." He led them down into the boat and Emily was surprised with how much room there was. The main living area had a small kitchen and bench style dinette with a built-in couch across from it. Tim showed them the two bedrooms at the back of the boat and then went back to the stairs and opened a door beside them that led into another small bedroom. He finally turned to the side and opened a door that led into a tiny bathroom that had a toilet and the smallest shower that Emily had ever seen.

Lisa brushed past them and with another flirty smile, shut the bathroom door in Tim's face.

"Oh, right! Sorry, forgot you had to go. Just take it easy on the water. We don't have much and we have to conserve it," he yelled through the door.

Emily thought she heard a muffled "Whatever" from behind the door and suggested they go back up and see if the boys had returned. The last thing she wanted was for Tim to see Lisa's true colors and change his mind before they had even left the marina.

The boys hadn't returned yet so Emily tried to get to know Tim better. "This is a pretty big boat for one person, isn't it?" she asked.

"Yeah, it really is. I should have bought something smaller a while ago but I'm sentimental about the Lawless. My dad helped me buy it when I was nineteen. She was a wreck with so much damage that I didn't think she'd ever float, let alone sail. But the price was right and he convinced me it would be a good project for the two of us. It took us two years just to get her on water and then another couple of years to outfit her properly. I've been sailing her for the past six years and have really come to love the big girl. The thing is, if I had traded her for something else, it would have been full of bells and whistles that would all be dead right now. So it's a really good thing I kept her or we'd all be paddling a dinghy north."

Emily nodded her agreement. "I can't thank you enough for this. The things we saw on the way here…it was horrible. I can only imagine how much worse it's going to get. I don't think we would have made it out alive."

Tim nodded thoughtfully. "I agree, this city is going to burn. Anyway, with all the supplies you guys have, it won't be a burden for me to help you out. It will actually make things a little easier on me if Mason can help out some. And it'll be a nice change to have some company. It's a long couple of weeks to get up to Seattle so I'm glad to have you aboard." He smiled reassuringly.

The sound of engines could be heard so they both moved over to the dock and saw the three golf carts heading their way. The boys parked and jumped out. Immediately, they started to unload the supplies from the back and passed them up to Tim and Emily. The deck started to fill up quickly so Emily started to carry things down into the cabin. On her fourth trip down, the living area had boxes and bags stacked everywhere and David followed her down with two cases of water.

As he passed her he asked, "You okay?"

She pushed her sweaty hair out of her eyes and nodded. "I can't wait to get out of here. How much more is there to unload?"

"We have everything aboard now. Tim, Mason and Mark just took two of the carts to scavenge from the restaurant. He wants us to try some of the closer boats for gas cans or other things we might be able to use." David stretched his back after lowering the two cases of water and looked around. "Where's Lisa?"

Emily froze for a minute. She couldn't believe she had forgotten about the girl. Her head slowly swiveled towards the bathroom door. "Lisa?" she called. When she didn't get an answer, she went to the door and was about to knock when the door opened. Emily's jaw dropped. She couldn't believe her eyes. Lisa stood in front of her with her eye brows raised while she continued to dry her hair. She was naked except for a towel wrapped around her torso. Emily had to back away and close her eyes. She took deep breaths and tried to push her anger down. This…this stupid fool had had a shower!

David was looking at Emily in confusion. He stepped forward to see into the bathroom and a look of disgust crossed his face at the sight of a dripping Lisa.

"Are you really that stupid?" he asked her in surprise. "We need that water to live on. How much did you just waste?"

"What is your damage? I was so sweaty and gross from the walk here. I needed to get cleaned up. We have plenty of bottled water to drink," she said nastily.

David shook his head in disbelief, "We could be on this boat for three weeks or more. Those cases of water won't be enough! No one can have a shower! We can't waste any more water!"

"Oh my God! Could you be any more of a drama queen?" she said with a roll of her eyes.

Emily couldn't take anymore. She stepped right up to Lisa and put her face close to hers. "I will not die because of you. If you do one more stupid, selfish, shallow thing, I will personally throw you overboard. I am not joking, Lisa. If it means you have to go so that the rest of us will live, I will do it." she hissed through clenched teeth.

David pulled her away from Lisa and looked to her. "She still doesn't get it, Em, and she won't until she's dying from dehydration. Lisa, don't use any more water. Get dressed, now. You'll help us search the other boats for supplies and keep your mouth shut or Tim might decide you're too much trouble to take with us." He didn't wait for her response. He just pushed Emily ahead of him and up the stairs.

Up on deck, Emily was shaking from anger and fear. All she could think about was Alex. She would do anything to go back to the start of this day and change her decision. She and David should have gone with them. She rubbed her face with her hands and tried to keep the tears from falling.

Chapter 5

David finished carrying everything down into the cabin and returned with a now dressed Lisa. The girl wouldn't look at Emily as she went past and down the ladder to the dock. After they had all climbed down, David waved them into the last golf cart and they drove to the next dock of boats. Tim had told him that he had already searched the closest boats and to start further away. He parked halfway down the dock so they wouldn't have to carry the supplies that they found so far.

"Keep your ears open, girls. We haven't seen anyone here yet but that doesn't mean that no one is onboard one of these boats. We are running out of time so we should split up. Emily, you and Lisa take the right side and I'll take the left. I got a couple of crowbars from the golf course. Do you think you can force the cabin doors open?"

Emily reached out and took the tool with a nod.

"Okay, look for gas cans. The more we have, the further we will get when we need to use the engine. Also, grab any water and food, first aid kits, any stuff that you think will come in handy. Let's move as fast as we can but be careful." He glanced at Lisa meaningfully before continuing. "I know we need all we can find but just stick to the yachts without sails. Those owners will probably not try to get here but the sailboats owners could still get out so let's leave their stuff, okay?"

"Yes, that's a good idea, David. I would hate to think of a family who had a chance to get out of this city suffering because we stole their stuff."

Without looking at Lisa, Emily turned and headed down the row of boats to a huge power yacht. She climbed the ladder awkwardly with the crowbar and stepped up onto the deck. There was nothing out in the open so she headed straight for the cabin door. It took four tries, but she managed to get the door open and she was sweating from the effort. Emily ignored Lisa, who was standing behind her, waiting for the hard work to be done.

"What a useless waste of space," Emily thought to herself.

The inside of the cabin was dim and she went over to the windows and pulled back the curtains. Emily turned to open the curtains on the other side of the cabin and was surprised to see Lisa already pulling them open. The girl turned and caught Emily's surprised expression.

"What? I know you think I'm useless but I'm not brain-dead you know," she said sarcastically.

"Then stop acting like you are, Lisa," Emily countered.

Lisa's lips pressed flat together and she looked down at the floor. "Look, I'm sorry about the shower, okay. I didn't think about the water issue. This isn't exactly familiar territory for me."

Emily studied Lisa's frowning face. She was surprised that the girl had apologised and forced herself to soften a little. They were all out of their comfort zones and if she could forgive Mason for his actions then she should be able to ease up on Lisa too.

"Listen, Lisa, I'm sorry I got so mad at you. It's just that I'm so scared right now, and this situation is really serious. We have to make smarter choices if we're going to survive. I meant what I said earlier. We've got to work as a team no matter how we feel about each other. It's the only way we'll get home. None of us are exactly in familiar territory here. We've got to really think about what we are doing so we don't make mistakes. Everything is different now. All the things that used to matter don't anymore. Just try and make smarter choices, okay? You can't just think about yourself because…we're all in the same boat together," she finished with a grin.

Lisa had been staring at the floor while Emily talked but at the pun she looked up and gave a half laugh.

"Oh, that's so bad. Funny, but bad." Her smile faded. "I just wanted to say thanks for taking care of me back on the street, after the shooting. I was terrified."

Emily reached out and gave her arm a squeeze. "Yeah, me too. Come on, let's see what we can find."

They searched eight boats and came away with a surprisingly large amount of food and water. Every boat had gas cans with extra fuel and they piled them on the deck for David to load in the cart. By the time they had finished their golf cart was full and there was a huge pile still to be loaded on the dock. Mason pulled up with another cart and helped load the rest. The two carts were so overloaded that Lisa and Emily had to walk back to the Lawless.

By the time they made it back, Tim and the boys were just finishing loading everything onboard and the sun was almost down. The girls climbed onboard and Emily surveyed the piles of supplies everywhere. She was so tired from the long day and her arms ached from prying open cabin doors and hauling so many heavy items. She couldn't help the groan that escaped when she reached down and lifted two one gallon jugs of water. They had to clear the deck and secure all of this before they got under way. She carried the water down the stairs and shot Lisa an understanding smile over her shoulder when her groan followed. They had seemed to have declared a truce and she was happy that Lisa was doing more to help out.

Tim was in the cabin organising and he showed them all the cupboards and hidey holes to put supplies in. The girls took over stowing supplies and Tim went back up on deck to finish getting ready to sail. It was twilight when the girls finished and came back up on deck. Emily looked towards the city and was saddened that the miles and miles of lights she had seen the night before were now dark.

"I think we've got everything secure in the cabin, Tim." Emily reported.

Tim looked over to see make sure David was finished tying down everything that had to be stowed on deck. "Okay, thanks. Let's get going then. Mason, cast off."

Tim started the motor and Mason threw off the lines. As they slowly made their way out of the marina, Emily shivered. They were safe from the lawless and chaos-filled city but what would find them out in the open water? She was happy they were on their way but nervous as well. If something happened out on the ocean, there would be no rescue and nowhere to run. Once again she found herself wishing they had gone overland with Alex. Just then, Mason came over to her side and put his arm around her. She leaned against him and closed her eyes. She silently prayed for their safety and hoped that she could count on this boy who claimed to love her.

The gasps and exclamations of the others made her open her eyes and look around. She let out a sob at the view. They were out of the marina and heading out to open water but it was the receding shoreline that everyone was looking at. The city lights might have been out, but there were many red glows over it. The further away they got, the more of the city they could see and it was devastating. Smaller fires were everywhere and several huge blazes seemed to expand in seconds.

She met David's eyes across the boat and knew they were thinking the same thing. "Do you think they made it out?" she asked him.

He nodded firmly. "Quinn and Josh would have pushed them hard to clear it by now. They're out Em, I know it. Don't know about the rest of them though. Mrs. Moore is pretty forceful but she had a lot working against her. I just don't know how they could survive in that." He looked back at the burning city.

Emily closed her eyes again and let the cool ocean breeze dry the tears from her face as she sent a prayer up for her teacher and all the other students that chose to stay. She knew in her heart she would never see them again.

They all stayed that way, standing on the deck of the boat watching the faint outlines of the city in the red glow of fires until it got too far away to see. Emily looked around at the faces of her companions in the dim glow of the two lanterns that were secured to both ends of the deck. Everyone's faces were lined with exhaustion from the harrowing day. Mark was leaning against the mast and he seemed to be sleeping on his feet. Tim cleared his throat and had to raise his voice slightly to be heard over the wind.

"You guys should all go below and get some sleep. I'm going to put the sails up in a minute and its best if you were out of the way until I get you guys trained up. You girls can share the main bedroom and the four of us guys can rotate the other two beds. I'll be up here all night so sack out and I'll see you in the morning."

Everyone started shuffling towards the stairs and down below. Emily stopped beside Tim. "Can I make you some coffee or get you anything?" she asked him.

"Thanks, kid, but I've got a little cooler here with some Coke that will keep me going. You look beat, get some sleep." He ushered her away with a nice smile.

Emily could barely keep her eyes open. She knew she was hungry - they had hardly eaten more than energy bars and beef jerky all day but she was in no condition to make herself or anyone else anything. Stumbling down the stairs, she used the bathroom and wondered briefly about toothbrushes but decided tomorrow was soon enough. She was grateful for the small bit of light coming through the windows from the lanterns on deck so that she didn't trip in the unfamiliar area. She had almost passed the couch when her hand was grabbed by what she thought was another heaped pile of supplies. She realized that David was sprawled out on the couch and guessed he had given the beds up to Mason and Mark. He gave her hand another squeeze and let it go.

"Night, Em," he muttered sleepily.

"Night, David." She stepped towards the bedroom but stopped and turned back. Leaning down over him, she kissed his forehead and whispered, "Thanks for coming with me," and went to her and Lisa's room, closing the door. She didn't have the energy to undress so she just lay down on top of the covers fully clothed.

As Emily felt the strain in her body ease away, she thought about David. She had been so wrapped up in her own fears and worries that she had hardly even thought of his. She was so grateful that he had joined them but she hadn't thought about how hard it would be on him. She at least had Mason but David had no friends in this group but her. As she slipped into sleep, she wondered if he regretted coming with them and was wishing he had gone overland as well.

** ** ** ** ** ** ** ** ** **

Emily couldn't breathe or see, the smoke was so thick. Everything around her was burning and every now and then it would clear enough that she could see dead bodies everywhere. She ran screaming for her friends but she couldn't find them, just endless smoke and flames, her feet tripping over bloody bodies as she ran. She stopped and spun around, looking for anyone who could help but when the wind blew the smoke away, she found herself facing two smirking men in baggy jeans and wife beater tank tops. The taller man snarled and said, "Here's another one!" as he raised his hand and pointed at her. Emily gasped as she saw the gun pointed at her head and screamed herself awake to the sound of the gunshot.

She was shaking and drenched in sweat from the nightmare. The cabin was filled with muted sunlight that was filtered from the curtains covering the deck windows. She was alone in the bed and she flinched at another bang from the main room. Emily realized that it was someone banging cupboard doors in the galley that had woken her. Someone was walking around on the deck and the sounds of puking were very clear. Scrubbing her sweaty face with her hands, she swung down from the bed and opened the door to see what was going on.

Tim was going through all the cupboards looking for something and sent her a distracted smile when he noticed her in the doorway.

"Hey, sorry if I woke you, but we seem to be having a pukefest on deck and I'm looking for the Dramamine. Mark and Lisa are hanging over the edge and it's not a pretty sight. How are you feeling?" he asked with a frown at her tired and sweaty face.

"I'm fine, just a nightmare. Grab some crackers as well. It will help if they had something in their stomachs. I'm going to get cleaned up and I'll be right up." Emily flashed him a wan smile and headed to the tiny bathroom.

She stopped at a pile of clothes and sorted through them for the things she had gotten at Costco. Looking around the cabin at things tossed everywhere she decided it would be a good thing to sort everything and put it all away after she had cleaned herself up. In the bathroom, she found the boxes of toothbrushes and sighed in relief. Under the sink, she found washcloths and soap. Using very little water, Emily stripped her clothes off and washed her body as best as she could. She couldn't help but be jealous that Lisa had showered yesterday. Her scalp was itchy and her hair smelled like smoke.

Putting on fresh clothes helped a lot and after brushing her long blond hair she knotted it high up on the back of her head. Without makeup, there was nothing she could do about the dark bags under her eyes so she settled for a layer of sunscreen and called it good. Stepping back out into the cabin her stomach gave a lurch and she remembered how long it had been since she had eaten. Emily searched around until she found the instant oatmeal and made herself a bowl with bottled water. She left it sitting on the counter to soak and started to move stuff around. There hadn't been much time last night to stow everything properly and the cabin was a mess. She worked away at it for ten minutes before she started to feel nauseous so she grabbed her bowl and started to eat. It was awful made from cold water but she ate it anyway. Her belly felt a little better when she was done so she put the bowl in the sink and went back to work on the cabin.

Mason came down the stairs as she worked and he grabbed a granola bar and watched her. Emily still wasn't sure about him after what happened yesterday so she just ignored him. After a few minutes he let out an exaggerated sigh.

"Are you going to give me the cold shoulder for the whole trip home?"

"I'm not giving you the cold shoulder, Mason. I'm just…thinking things through. That's all," she told him without looking at him.

It was true. She didn't know how she felt about him anymore. His leaving her on the street blew every ounce of trust she had with him. Saying that he loved her made things even worse, as she couldn't believe that you would abandon someone you loved. So, either he was lying, or he didn't really know what love was, and that was something she needed to really think about. She turned around and faced him and her heart softened at how miserable he looked.

"Mason, I just need a little time to figure things out. You really scared me yesterday. I just don't know how I feel right now. Just be there for me, okay? We'll get through this together." She let him fold her into his arms and she felt a little bit better. The sounds of someone retching on deck made her pull back.

"Tim said Lisa and Mark are seasick. Are they okay? He was going to give them some medicine," Emily asked with concern.

"Yeah, he tried but they both threw it back up. It's pretty gross. David seems fine. How about you?"

"I'm okay. I had something to eat and that helped a lot. Help me clean this place up some more and we can get them down here. If they aren't looking at the waves they might feel better."

"Good idea. We'll get them some puke buckets and leave them alone to be miserable together. We can go up and enjoy the sun," he said with a smirk.

Emily had to shake her head at him. Sometimes he was such a jerk. They finished organizing the cabin and Emily lined two waste paper baskets with plastic bags, put a box of crackers on the table and two bottles of water in the cup holders. From the bathroom, she wet two washcloths and brought them out to the table as well. Mason went up on deck and helped Lisa down. She collapsed at the table and rested her head in her hands with a moan. She was so pale and her eyes were sunken. Mark came down and settled across from her. The shade of sickly green his skin had changed to didn't look very good with his red hair. Emily placed the baskets next to them and handed them both the cool washcloths.

"Try and eat some crackers, guys. It will help with the nausea and once they stay down you can have some medicine that will make it much better."

Neither one of them even acknowledged her so she left them alone and went up on deck for the first time that day. The sun was brilliant and the air was clean. There was no taint of smoke in the wind and she tilted her head back and let the wind blow over her face.

Looking around on deck she saw Tim at the wheel and Mason and David sitting back enjoying the sun. There were resting places moulded into the deck so she lowered herself into one and just let the stress of their situation go for a few moments. Mason scooted closer to her and handed her a bottle of water. He draped his arm over her shoulder and she leaned into him. They sat like that for ten minutes until Tim spoke and brought their attention to him.

"There's another one. How many does that make, David?" he asked, pointing out ahead of them.

David grabbed the binoculars and stood to take a look. "That makes six. It's a big one too."

"What is it? What are you guys talking about?" Emily asked while trying to see into the distance.

"Dead ships. We've seen trawlers, oil tankers, cargo ships. We even saw a small cruise ship. They're all stranded out here," Tim told her.

"That's terrible, all those people so far from shore! What are we going to do?" she asked him.

Tim looked at her and frowned sadly. "There's nothing we can do, Emily. We couldn't take on very many people and if we tried we would just end up swamped. All those ships have lifeboats. They'll have to try for land pretty soon. If rough weather comes up and they don't have any power, most of those ships will go down. Things are going to be just as bad out here as on land, just more spread out. We have to keep going if we want to make it."

Emily dropped her head in defeat. Knowing he was right didn't make her heart ache any less for all the pain and death the world was going through. It would be easy to forget what was happening on land while out in the ocean but she knew they would have to face it once they docked again. She took the binoculars from David and scanned the seas all around them, focusing on the huge ship that was off in the distance. She thought she could see tiny people on the deck waving their arms. She turned to David to mention it when her stomach dropped and she had to rush to the side where all her breakfast came rushing out. David held onto her while she heaved again and again until there was nothing left. He helped her to the stairs and down below where she joined the others in their misery.

Chapter 6

The next three days were hell for Emily and everyone else onboard. She seriously thought she would die. Nothing would stay down and even when her belly was empty she continued to dry heave. Lisa and Mark were just as bad off as she was and Mason and David had their hands full trying to take care of them. Tim had stopped trying to give them the small amount of medicine he had onboard as they just threw it up before it could even take effect. Her throat was raw, and her abdomen muscles ached like she had been punched repeatedly. It helped to be up on deck where they could see the horizon but there just wasn't room for all of them to be up there comfortably. Those three days were a blur for Emily and all she wanted was her mom's cool hand on her forehead.

Tim tried to help but he had his hands full sailing the boat and teaching Mason as much as he could. It was the fourth night on the boat and the three patients were slumped around the table when Tim came flying down the stairs with a look of triumph on his face.

"I'm so sorry I didn't think of this before guys. I know how to get the medicine into you." He raced into the bathroom and came out with the bottle of Dramamine.

Mark groaned and muttered, "Save it."

Lisa and Emily just shook their heads. They had all tried to keep the medicine down but it just wouldn't work.

"No, really! I just remembered a friend telling me this trick. It will work, I know it. You guys really need to get some fluids and food in you, as well as a good night sleep. Take one of these pills and put it under your tongue. Let it dissolve fully. Don't try and swallow it. It's going to taste really bad but it will finally get into your system and start to work," he explained while handing out the pills.

Emily was willing to try anything to get this under control. She was feeling really weak and her head pounded from dehydration. The pill was very bitter and her tongue started to go numb but she kept it there until it had dissolved. After twenty minutes, she took a cautious sip of water and waited. After a few more sips, she tried a cracker and then another one. One hour after they had taken the pills, all three felt much better. They all felt drowsy but Tim wouldn't let them sleep until they had all had a bowl of soup and more water.

Emily barely remembered crawling into bed next to Lisa. Her only thought was to wonder what would be for breakfast.

When Emily cracked her eyes open the next morning, she stayed perfectly still taking stock of her body. She felt clear-headed for the first time in days and knew she had turned a corner. She turned her head slightly and saw the bottle of medicine in the cup holder beside the bed, slowly reached out for it and got it open. She felt Lisa shift beside her and cautiously turned her head to see that Lisa was awake and staring at the ceiling. Neither girl wanted to move in case the sickness came rushing back. Emily slipped one of the pills into the other girl's hand and whispered to her.

"Put it under your tongue. Let's just stay here until we know it's going to work."

"It has to work. I can't do that again. I don't endorse anorexia as a diet plan," Lisa whimpered jokingly.

Emily laughed. It was the first time she had heard Lisa make a joke that wasn't full of nasty sarcasm. They laid side by side waiting for the pills to dissolve and take effect. After a while they could hear someone banging around in the kitchen. Soon the smell of cooking came to them and Emily's belly growled loudly.

Lisa's head whipped towards her and she had panic on her face. "Oh God, are you going to hurl?"

Emily lay frozen; she just couldn't take being sick again. After a few minutes, she turned her head towards Lisa and slowly smiled. "I think…I'm hungry. And judging by the smell I think that someone is cooking pancakes. Do you want to get up?"

Lisa's concerned face changed to one of relief and she smiled while nodding her head. "Oh yeah, let's go. I swear if breakfast stays down I'm going to lay on the deck and suntan all day long."

The girls cautiously got up and got dressed. When Lisa held the door open for Emily, she marveled that it had taken a pukefest to get them past their animosity towards each other. Tim was in the kitchen using the small propane stove and he was expertly flipping pancakes onto a growing stack. When he saw the girls come out of the bedroom, his face blossomed with relief.

"Ladies, you both look so much better! I hope your appetites have returned. You both need to make up the calories that you lost the past few days. I found a huge bag of just add water pancake mix so fill your plates. We don't have any butter or maple syrup but we have jam and peanut butter so they'll still be good."

The girls grabbed plates and helped themselves from the stack. They sat at the dining table and smeared their pancakes with the breakfast condiments waiting there. Emily made a sandwich with hers and happily munched her way through her plate. When she had finished she let out an uncontrollable yawn. "This is crazy. I could go right back to sleep," she muttered.

Lisa added her own yawn. Emily realized that the medication was taking effect and they were feeling the side effects.

"So the upside is we won't be throwing up constantly but the downside is all we'll want to do is sleep. Can't seem to win this one," she told Lisa.

"I can live with that. I have no problem napping while working on my tan. It's not like we have a lot to do for the next couple of weeks. It's probably a good thing if you think about it. You said when we land that we'll have to walk the rest of the way home, so we should rest up while we can, right?" Lisa asked.

"That is true. We are so lucky Tim's helping us. Where do you think Alex and others are? I can't even imagine how bad it must be for them right now. I wonder if they found bikes or a ride. It's been what? Five days since it happened. How far do you think they've gotten?" Emily wondered with a frown.

Tim sat down at the table with them and started to fix his pancakes. "Who are you talking about, Emily?" he asked while rolling up his jam-filled pancake.

"There were ten of us that decided to get out of the city that day. Our teacher told us what she thought had happened and encouraged us to try and get out of the city. My best friend Alex and some of the others wanted to go overland. But Mason convinced us that finding a boat out would be a better idea. We split up and went our different ways," she told him sadly.

Tim seemed to consider this. "Well, if they made it out of the city, they would have a very hard road ahead of them. They would have to get over the mountains first and then they'd have to cross the desert." He shook his head. "I don't think anyone could make that trip on foot. Even if they had bikes it would be next to impossible. Sorry, Emily."

David had come down from the deck while Tim was talking. He was shaking his head with a fierce expression. "You don't know my friends. Quinn and Josh will make it happen and Alex doesn't know the meaning of quit. I believe a hundred percent that they will make it. I have no doubt," he said with confidence.

Tim waved David towards the stack of waiting pancakes and waited while he fixed his plate before speaking. "You're right. I don't know your friends and if they're as smart as you guys, they probably have a pretty good shot. I mean, look what your group did. You guys walked over twenty miles through a burning city filled with gunshots and mayhem. You found transportation and managed to fill them with a huge amount of supplies and made it to the marina. So you're right, David, they have a good chance." He smiled reassuringly at Alex and continued, "It's good in a way that it will take us a few more weeks to get back to land. I know this is going to sound harsh but we have to be prepared. The first week will be bad with all the confusion but most people will have had some food and water on hand. The second week people will start getting really desperate and that's when things will get the ugliest. Massive amounts of people will start leaving the cities and larger towns. They'll head out to the country looking for food and water. There will be a huge die off as people who haven't walked further than from their cars to their offices start making extreme physical demands on their bodies. People will die from exhaustion, exposure and dehydration. Violence will take out a lot of people as they fight over dwindling resources. Anyone who is dependent on modern medicine and drugs will die as well. In the third week, disease will start to crop up. All those bodies lying around will be rotting. When we hit land, it will be important to stay away from any population centers. Stick to fields and forested areas. You'll have to watch out for survivors who are going to be ready to shoot first to try and protect any supplies they have left. My family has a cabin up in the Cascades that I'm going to head for. You guys will have a much longer hike to get up into B.C. David, we'll take a look at those maps you have later and try to plot a route. Anyway, there will be a lot less people around by the time we have to start walking."

The table was filled with silence as they all digested the gruesome picture that Tim had painted. Emily thought about her family and felt tears welling in her eyes. She ruthlessly pushed those thoughts back. She couldn't let herself speculate on their well-being or she would dissolve in grief.

One of the bedroom doors crashed open and Mark stumbled out. He staggered over to the table and dropped heavily down onto the bench. Tim asked him how he felt but all he got in return was a grunt as Mark started to shove food into his mouth. He had had the worst time of the sickness, and he looked horrible. His face was haggard, and it was plain to see he had lost weight. Mark's red hair was greasy and matted and the smell coming off him was rank. Emily was more than ready to escape up onto the deck into the fresh air. Thoughts of being on deck made Emily's head whip towards Tim.

"Tim, shouldn't you be sailing the boat?" she asked with wide eyes.

He laughed, "Don't worry, Mason's got it. While you guys were out of it, I've been teaching him as much as I can. He's a fast learner and right now there are clear skies and good wind so all he really needs to do is stay on course and keep an eye out. You're right though, I should head on up and take over so he can have something to eat."

With a brief frown towards Mark, he jumped up and put his plate in the sink and disappeared up the stairs. Emily, Lisa and David were quick to follow him. Mark didn't even seem to notice he had been left alone as he stuffed another pancake into his mouth.

It was another brilliantly clear day on the water. Emily loved the feel of the fresh wind blowing through her hair. Mason's face broke into a huge smile when he saw her come up the stairs. She went to him and he pulled her close to his side.

"You feel better! I was really starting to worry about you, Em. This is amazing. I love being out here on the water. We can just relax and forget about all the crap that's happening on land."

Emily frowned at that. It was easier being out on the ocean but she couldn't forget about the pain and suffering happening especially not knowing if her family and friends were okay.

"It is nice, Mason but this isn't a vacation. Aren't you worried about your family?"

He laughed. "Oh, I'm sure they're fine. My dad will just bull his way through anything. You know what he's like. He probably bullied someone to get the house stocked on the first day. He's got his hunting rifles and I'm sure Brett's made it home by now. Besides, there's nothing to worry about in central Alberta, lots of farms and cattle to feed everyone. Don't worry so much. Just relax and get a tan." He bent down to kiss her head and made a face. "You should get cleaned up, wash your hair. You've been sick for days and you would feel much better if you did." He let go of her and put his hand back on the wheel.

Emily stepped away from him in embarrassment. She knew she wasn't looking or smelling her best but that wasn't exactly her fault. Maybe she should ask Tim to stop the boat so she could take a dip in the ocean and scrub off. The salt water would be better than being stinky. Tim noticed Emily's embarrassment and intervened.

"Hey Emily, we're looking pretty good for water in the tank. You can have a fast shower if you want. Just get in and get wet, turn the water off and soap up and then rinse. If you do it that way, it doesn't actually use that much water."

Emily looked at Tim with excitement, "Really? Oh, wow, that would be great! I was contemplating going for a swim to clean off."

He laughed "We might have to resort to that but not yet. I know you'll be conservative with the water so go ahead."

Lisa was just as excited about the prospects of a shower and she started to follow Emily down into the cabin until Tim called her back. "Lisa, we need to go over some shower rules first, please."

Emily heard her groan as she left her there on deck. She quickly gathered up her cleanest clothes and a towel and headed to the tiny bathroom. Mason had followed her down and intercepted her at the door.

"Hey, why don't we really conserve water and I'll join you in there. I could scrub your back," he offered.

Emily just stared at him with a bland expression until he backed away. "Okay, okay, just thought we could have some fun," he muttered.

She watched him sit at the table and grab some food before closing herself into the bathroom. Emily shook her head at her reflection. She wasn't sure if she even wanted to be Mason's girlfriend anymore let alone have some "fun" with him. She turned away from her hollow-looking eyes and stripped off her clothes.

Mason was eating moodily. He thought about how distant Emily had been with him and tried to think of how he could bring her around. Mark snorted in laughter bringing Mason's head up to meet his friend's eyes.

"You're never going to crack that safe, man. You're going to have to tap the reserves," he said with a smirk. Mason looked around quickly to make sure no one was around.

"Give it time. We're going to be out here for a couple more weeks. It'll happen," he said confidently. Looking his friend over, Mason made a face. "Man, you're rank. Tim says we can have showers if we do the stop and start method. You could really use one. I could smell you up on deck."

Mark laughed "It's seasoning, man, but yeah, I'll get cleaned up. So how have things been while I was in pukeland? How's the Boy Scout?"

Mason shook his head, "David's not bad. He's actually a pretty good guy. He's always up for helping out. He doesn't talk much but he's okay. Tim's been teaching me a lot. The more I learn the better. I'm thinking after we land in Washington, we stick around until he's gone and "borrow" the boat to take us up into B.C. It will save us weeks of walking," he told Mark quietly.

Mark nodded thoughtfully, "Let's keep that on the down low for now. We don't need the Boy Scout knowing our plans."

Mason agreed, David seemed like an okay guy but he was a little too nice for this new world and he'd have to toughen up if he wanted a ride up into Canada. He dumped his plate into the full sink and headed back up on deck passing Lisa as she came down for her turn in the shower.

Mark looked her up and down and smirked. "Hey there, princess, it looks like you've lost some of the shine from your crown."

Lisa glared at him. "Could you be anymore disgusting, Mark? Really, you should grab the next shower. I just stopped puking and the smell coming off of you is about to start me heaving again," she said with disgust and quickly went into the bedroom and slammed the door.

Mark stared at the closed door and brooded. Lisa had always treated him like crap and he'd taken it but this was a brand new world they were in and the rules had changed. He had always been in Mason's shadow, the popular quarterback's sidekick. Mark knew he wasn't good looking or talented enough to be popular so sticking close to Mason in school was a no-brainer. He got all the benefits of being in the popular crowd without having to do any work, but all that was over now. It no longer mattered what crowd you were in. All that mattered was being strong and smart and ruthless. He planned on being all those things and more. He would deal with Mason as long as they needed this boat but after that he was going to learn that he wasn't number one anymore. As for Lisa, if she wanted to live, she would need to prove her worth to him. A small satisfied smile spread across Mark's face as he thought about his future.

Chapter 7

The next two days were uneventful. They played cards to pass the time or stayed on deck in the sun relaxing. Emily, Tim and David took turns making meals in the small galley. It was no surprise to find out that none of the others could cook. She found herself organizing and inventorying the supplies again and again. She couldn't stop thinking about what was to come once they docked. Knowing that they couldn't just go get food in a store made her nervous and she knew that all the stores would be picked clean by the time they got back to land. David and Tim pored over the maps that he had gotten at the gas station plotting the best routes through Washington State to the Canadian border. Mason didn't seem to be all that interested in the maps and Emily thought he was trusting David with it. Mark did nothing. He hardly talked to anyone, but Emily could see him watching everything. It gave her the creeps every time she felt his eyes on her. She used to just think Mark was a mean bully but lately she felt something more menacing coming from him. She tried to stay away from him and she noticed Lisa did as well.

Lisa had reverted back to her sarcastic attitude and the common ground between the two girls seemed to be lost. She spent most of her time on deck working on her tan, wearing a bikini she had found in Tim's closet. When she had emerged on deck in the small white suit two days ago, all the guys had stared, making Lisa toss her hair and pose like a model.

"I hope you don't mind, Tim, I found this in the back of your closet and since I didn't bring my own I borrowed it," she said with a flirty smile.

"Um, yeah...ok, sure. I mean, no problem. It was probably left by one of my exes." He shook his head in amusement.

David looked at Emily and just shrugged before turning back to the wide expanse of ocean ahead of them. Mason was openly staring at her and Mark had a creepy leer on his face. Emily shook her head in disgust at the boys and went and sat with David.

She hadn't really talked to him since they had set sail. She shoulder bumped him and he gave her a smile.

With a sad sigh, she asked him, "What do you think is happening at home?"

He turned his gaze back out to the ocean and frowned. "I don't know but I'm sure all of our families are okay. They would be looking out for each other and banding together to get things done. They're in a really good location. There are lots of farms and the forest for hunting and all the lakes for fishing. They're far enough from the cities that they shouldn't get too many people walking in. I just wish I was there to help. More than anything though, I'm mad."

Emily waited patiently for him to explain. Without taking his eyes off the view ahead he continued. "I'm stuck hundreds of miles from home; mom and Emma are alone and where the hell is my dad? Who knows where! He should be home taking care of them right now. Sometimes I hate him," he finished in a small sad voice.

There was nothing Emily could say to make him feel better about his dad so she just took his hand and gave it a squeeze. She had never met David's father and from what she had heard over the years, David barely knew him either. His father was a soldier and was away for most of David's younger years. He had been in Bosnia and Sarajevo where he had seen some horrifying things. When he had finally come home for good, he had tried to be a family man and a good father to David and his sister Emma but it was a struggle. David had told of screaming nightmares and violent mood swings that scared his mom. After he had been home for a year, she couldn't take it anymore and asked him to either get help or leave. David's dad had chosen to leave his family.

"I don't know why it even bothers me," David stated. "He was never really there for us ever. Mom's so strong and she's always done everything herself but it just isn't fair! He should be there!" he said in frustration.

"I'm sorry, David. I wish things were different for you guys," Emily said with compassion.

"Yeah, me too." David turned and looked at her. "What about you? How are you holding up?"

"Truth? I'm scared. I mean, this is beautiful, and it's great that we aren't walking, but I can't stop thinking about what comes next. I'm really worried and the others don't seem to even care. It's like they are on some great holiday. I tried to talk to Mason about home and he just brushed it off like it's no big deal! Lisa's great one minute and then the next she's back to being a diva. Mark...he scares me a little bit," she confided.

David nodded. "I know what you mean. I tried to go over the maps with Mason and he wasn't even interested. It's like he plans on sailing all the way home. I don't know what to tell you about Lisa. It's almost like she doesn't know who she is. Sometimes she's funny and easy to talk to and then it's like she puts on this shallow girl act. I mainly just try and stay out of her way. I don't get Mark at all. He doesn't even talk to me except to make nasty comments but he's always watching us. It's almost like he's got some secret agenda and he's just waiting for the right time. I think you should stay away from him." He was quiet for a while and then tentatively asked, "What about you and Mason, are you guys still together?"

Emily looked down at her hands. "I just...I guess, I mean...I'm so confused! All the reasons that I liked him seem to have disappeared. He's not who I thought he was. I don't really believe that he loves me but I don't know what to do! This is a pretty small boat to have to deal with the fallout of a breakup. I guess I'll just keep things the same for now and hope for the best." She laughed ruefully. "We have so much to worry about like what's going on at home and how we'll get there once we land, that breaking up with my boyfriend seems pretty petty in comparison."

David smiled, "Yeah, I guess normal teenage stuff's going to have to take a backseat for a while. I don't think we should talk about it right now but I think we should consider splitting up when we do hit land. I'm just not sure we can count on those guys and we can't afford to make stupid mistakes. Think about it, okay?"

Emily nodded, just one more thing to worry about.

** ** ** ** ** ** ** ** ** **

They had been on the boat for seven days and Emily was in the main bedroom reading one of Tim's paperback books. It was a very boring mystery but she was desperate for something to take her mind off of her worries as well as find a little bit of privacy. It was hard to be alone with six people onboard and they had all tried to get away from each other at some point. Tim seemed the least bothered and he was very good natured. He always seemed to find humor and was never testy with them. He was such a great guy and Emily was grateful to him for all he had done for them. She just wished that there was something she could do to keep busy. Emily had just reread the same page three times when she heard yelling coming from on deck. She threw the book aside and rushed out of the room and up the stairs to the deck to see what the commotion was all about.

David was looking out in the distance with the binoculars and Tim was busy dropping the sails to slow the boat down while Mason manned the wheel. She tried to see what David was looking at but the glare off the water made it too difficult. Lisa had lifted herself up onto her elbows from her tanning position but at Emily's shrug she laid back down, indifferent towards the situation. Tim brushed past her back to the wheel and within minutes, Emily felt the vibrations of the motor as it came to life. She made her way to David and tried to see what had captured his attention again. She thought she could make out something bobbing on the waves in the distance but couldn't make out what it was.

"What is it, David? What's out there?" she asked him.

Without taking his eyes off the object, he explained. "It's a lifeboat. I can't see anyone in it but they could be lying down in the bottom of it. We're going to try and get closer."

Emily felt a surge of apprehension. On one hand, it would be great if they could help other survivors but on the other hand, they only had so many supplies. She felt guilty at the thought but pushed it aside when she thought of being stuck in a lifeboat for days with no food or water and being at the mercy of the sea.

It seemed to take forever for the lifeboat to come into range. When it finally was close enough to see down into it, they could make out three men lying on the bottom that weren't moving. Tim had Mason take the wheel and he came towards Emily and David. He stopped and unclipped a long handled paddle that was in brackets under the cabins windows. As the lifeboat floated closer he reached out and tried to snag it in closer but missed. David helped Tim by wrapping his arms around his waist so he could safely reach out further. It worked but the paddle hit one of the men, pushing him over so he faced up. With a cry of horror, Tim and David stumbled back against the cabin leaving Emily with a perfect view down into the lifeboat. She was completely unprepared for what she saw.

The corpse of the man stared back at her. His face was a dark red and his skin had dried out and pulled away from his teeth making him look like he was smiling maniacally. His eyes were gone and the sockets had sunken deep leaving him with two dark holes. Emily was frozen in place staring at the poor man's face and she heard herself whimper.

"Man, that's sick!" came from behind her and the cruel amusement in the tone broke the spell and made her turn away from the ravaged face. She swallowed down the vomit that threatened to rise and looked to Tim and David. Mark was making disgusting comments about the state of the bodies when the wind blew a gust that was full of decomposing scent. The smell overcame Emily and she had to rush further down the rail to be sick over the side. Tim got control of himself and pushed Mark back out of the way.

"What the hell is wrong with you?" he screamed.

Tim was still holding the long handled paddle and he quickly used it to shove the lifeboat away from the Lawless. Once it was far enough away that he couldn't reach it anymore, he dropped the paddle onto the deck and rushed over to the wheel, shoving Mason out of the way. He brought the engine up and motored them away from the lifeboat. He kept taking big gulps of air and Emily had never seen him so pale.

Mason came up to her and threw his arm around her shoulder. "Was it really nasty?" he asked.

Emily shoved his arm away and snapped at him, "Yes, it was nasty because those men were dead!" She turned and looked at Mark with his smirk and Lisa still tanning like nothing had happened. "Can't you people get it through your shallow selfish little minds? This is real. It's not a movie or a video game or a freakin' vacation! Those men are dead and we could be next! You all think this is a big joke! Well, I'm scared and you should be too because being popular isn't going to keep you alive," she yelled at them before she had to rush to the rail to empty her stomach once again into the sea. She didn't think she would ever be able to get that poor man's face out of her head.

Mason came up behind her and rubbed her back. "Emily, I'm sorry. I didn't mean to make light of them. Everything's going to be okay. Don't be scar…" instead of finishing the word, he gasped.

Emily scrubbed the tears from her face and looked up at him to see what had surprised him. Mason was shading his eyes looking out past her in the ocean. She turned around to see what he was looking at and what came from her throat was an agonized moan. Her eyes scanned the way ahead and she had to stop counting at twelve when the tears blurred her vision. She pushed past Mason and stumbled back down the stairs. Emily couldn't bear to stay on deck as they sailed through the cemetery of lifeboats ahead.

Chapter 8

Emily was sitting at the dinette with her head
cushioned on her folded arms when she heard someone
come down the stairs half an hour later. She had heard the
engine shut down and guessed that Tim had switched back
to sail. The bang of a glass being slammed onto the
counter made her wearily raise her head. Tim had a bottle
of some sort of alcohol and he splashed two inches into the
glass. Capping the bottle he turned and leaned against the
counter. His eyes were haunted and a million miles away.
He finally tossed back the drink in one gulp and his eyes
focused on Emily. With a frown at her, he turned back to
the cupboard and got another glass and brought it to the
table. He sat across from her and filled both glasses with
another two inches and slid one across to her.

When Emily just stared at the glass, Tim told her,
"Shoot it back in one go, kid. Trust me, it will help a little.
Besides, it's a little bit of home for you. It's Crown Royal
whiskey, Canadian."

Emily had only drunk once in her life and the bottle
of peach schnapps she and Alex had experimented with
had left them both sick as dogs. She didn't know what type
of alcohol this brown stuff was but when the dead man's
face came back to her she didn't care. Throwing the drink
back quickly, she wheezed out a breath at the burn of it
going down. She leaned back as she felt the warmth of the
drink spread through her. Tim was sipping his drink and
his expression was dark.

"That was brutal," he said. "It's one thing to know
what's happening but to see it up close like that…" There
weren't words to describe how hard it was to see so he fell
silent. After a few minutes, he sighed and looked at Emily.
"You got some color back in your face. That's better.
We're going to have to toughen up, kid. Things are not
easy out here. I put it out of my mind for a while but we
just got a huge reminder of what we will be facing in
another eight days or so." He downed the rest of the drink
and contemplated the bottle before shaking his head and

~ 65 ~

putting it back in the cupboard. He settled back at the table and scrubbed his face with his hands. "Can I ask you something?" When Emily nodded, he continued. "What are you and David doing with those three? You guys just don't seem to fit in with them."

Emily had to clear her throat twice before she could talk. It felt like the alcohol had burned the lining from her throat. "You're right; we don't fit in with them. It's my fault we are with them. I've been dating Mason for the last few months. I think David came with us just to make sure I was okay. I can honestly say at this point that I was a fool. My best friend and the others in our group went overland. I told you about Alex, Quinn and Josh already. David and I have been friends with them since we were little. I really don't know why I started dating Mason. We really have nothing in common, not even our friends. He was just different from the rest of us and I thought I saw something more than the shallow popular quarterback that he portrays. I'm pretty sure I was wrong. So now David and I are stuck on a boat with them," she said miserably.

Tim was nodding his head, "In college, I dated this girl. She was all dark and moody and wore black all the time. We had absolutely nothing in common. I still don't know why I was with her except she was so different from my regular group of friends. Now that I'm older I can look back and see the truth. Popular, jock…diva? They're all just masks. It's just something people use to cover the fact that they are just as scared and lost as the rest of us. In this situation, it won't be long before you'll start seeing those masks disappear and then you'll see the true person underneath. What I do know is that you and David - you guys don't wear masks. You'll be okay." He patted her hand and with a smile climbed back up to take the wheel.

Emily stayed put and felt the pleasant buzz from the drink. She thought about what Tim had said and wondered if it was true. When she started to date Mason and they were alone or on the phone, he seemed so different than when he was with his friends. She wasn't sure if his good side was his mask or if the real Mason was the selfish jock she had first thought him to be. Lisa was a mystery as well. The funny, smart girl that had peeked through on the trip so far seemed to come and go. Every time she started to like the girl, Lisa would revert to the snobby, shallow diva she had always shown before. Mark…well, she didn't even want to know him at all. Emily sighed in frustration. The only thing she really knew was that David was her true friend and she could count on him no matter what.

As if her thoughts had summoned him, David stopped down the stairs and threw himself down onto the bench beside her. His face was blank but his eyes were haunted and far away. She took his hand gently and just held it. After a while, he turned to look at her.

"That's not going to happen to us, Em, not like that. It's time to get busy. We have to start thinking ahead, worst case scenarios. If we had to leave this boat in a hurry, we would be in a world of hurt so we are going to make sure that doesn't happen. Remember those backpacks I got back at the Costco? We are going to fill them up with water and food and anything else that we might need. There's an unopened box of big Ziploc bags in the closet and a box of garbage bags too. We will make sure everything is sealed up watertight and then I'll put all the backpacks into the garbage bags and tie them to the lifeboat container. If we have to leave the boat, they will go with us. What do you think?"

"I think we should get started. Thanks, David. I'm scared and uncertain and doing something proactive makes me feel more in control of what might happen." She took a deep breath and confessed, "I'm so sorry we didn't go with Alex and Quinn. I know you only came to help me so…I'm sorry but I'm also really thankful that you did."

The intense look in his eyes made her look down at their joined hands. "I'm going to get us home, Emily. That's a promise."

She nodded her head, "Let's get to work."

They got up from the table and removed the bench seat cushions. Underneath the cushions was a hinged lid that opened to reveal storage areas. David pulled out the five backpacks that he had stuffed into it. Emily saw more bottled water and other supplies and was once again relieved that they had managed to get so much from Costco. The only problem was when they landed, they wouldn't be able to haul very much. They laid out the packs in five areas and started to make separate piles of supplies that each one would hold. David grabbed the garbage bags and the box of large Ziploc bags and handed them to Emily.

"Start filling these with food like the pancake mix, rice and oatmeal packets. We want to take dried stuff that we just add water to. The water will weigh the most so no canned stuff. The beef jerky is already sealed so it should be fine. We should look through Tim's pots and try to find a small pot and pan. The smallest we can find to fit into the packs and maybe a few small plates and cups. We can distribute them so each pack has one of each and a spoon and fork," David explained to her while he opened each garbage bag and used them to line the insides of all the packs.

Once Emily had assembled all the food they would pack, she sat back and thought of what else they would need. She flashed back to the bodies in the lifeboat and jumped to her feet. In the closets she found hats and she picked out the ones with the widest brims. When she shoved some jackets to one side, she found two umbrellas and added them to her pile. In the bathroom, she grabbed the first aid kit they had brought and one of the huge bottles of sunscreen from the multi pack Lisa had added. She contemplated the big bulky bottle. It would be better if all the packs had some of everything, that way if one was lost they would still have some in the others. She grabbed more of the Ziploc bags and started to squeeze some lotion into each. She made sure they were sealed and added one to each of the piles. David checked each flashlight from the package he had gotten at the store and added extra batteries to Ziploc bags. There were only a few left in the box by the time they were done.

David and Emily sat back and surveyed the five piles of supplies. They both racked their brains to try and think of anything else they could add to help them survive.

"What about a change of clothes or blankets?" Emily asked David.

"Well, there is still room to add a few things but not much. We should ask the others to add some stuff. I want to ask Tim about a couple of things and see if he has a bag he wants to pack as well. I saw a couple of compasses in the desk drawer but I want to ask him before I just take one. I'm going to go up and tell him what we are doing and see what he says. Why don't you take another look around and see if you can find anything else we should pack." David got up off the floor and stepped around the growing piles as he headed towards the stairs. He was halfway up when Emily saw him back down and move to the side so Lisa could come down. Without a word to her, he went past and bounded up the stairs to the deck.

Lisa looked amazing with her skin a perfect golden tan from all her time sunbathing. She was wearing dark sunglasses and the bikini she had borrowed. She headed towards the bedroom and promptly tripped over one of the five piles. She caught herself before she fell and quickly snatched off her dark glasses so she could see. Squinting her eyes she took in the floor and zeroed in on Emily.

"Really, Emily, it's not like there's a lot of room down here. Do you have to spread your stuff everywhere?" she asked in a snarly tone.

Emily answered in the exact same tone Lisa had used. "Really Lisa, I'm working on saving your life so why don't you go and do something important…like your nails."

Lisa's nasty expression changed to a frown. "What are you talking about? What is all this stuff for?" she asked.

"You saw those lifeboats, didn't you? David and I are putting together backpacks full of supplies so if we have to leave the boat quickly, we won't end up like them."

Lisa squatted down and started to sift through one of the piles. Without looking at Emily she asked in a quiet voice, "You don't really think that could happen to us, do you?"

Emily sighed, "I don't know. I hope not but it just makes sense to be prepared just in case. Listen, do you have a spare outfit you can give me for your pack? There isn't a lot of room but we can take a change of clothes if we roll it up tight."

Lisa looked thoughtful as she looked up and nodded. "Yeah, I'll go get one right now. Um...thanks for thinking of this, Emily," she said and quickly stood and went to the bedroom.

Emily was pleasantly surprised by the girl's words. Again, Lisa was showing two different sides. She just wished Lisa would pick one and stick to it.

Lisa came back out of the bedroom quickly and was about to sit down beside Emily when Mason and Mark came down the stairs. Instead of sitting she dropped the rolled up clothes on the floor and turned and went back into the room and shut the door. Mason kneeled down and started to go through one of the piles and started to nod his head.

"David told us what you guys are up too. It's a good idea, Emily. I'll grab some clothes to put in my pack." He sent her a charming smile and disappeared into one of the smaller bedrooms.

Mark took in all the supplies on the floor and with a smirk on his face turned and went to the other small bedroom. Emily didn't know why the guy was such a creep but she was just glad he rarely talked to her.

Looking around the cabin, Emily tried to think of anything else they could use that wouldn't take up much space. They had food, water, first aid stuff and sun protection. She pictured them floating for days in a lifeboat and what that would be like. What was she missing...something they would need? With a groan it came to her and she jumped up and ran to the bathroom. In the small towel cabinet she found toilet paper and grabbed three rolls. The box of tampons she had gotten was still unopened and she wasn't due to start her period for another few days so she grabbed a few of them as well. Emily remembered what Lisa had said about her not getting a period and was grateful she wouldn't have to share them with her. The multi packs of deodorant and toothbrushes and paste were in the cabinet as well and she didn't think they would take up too much space so she added them to the growing pile.

Each roll of paper and the tampons went into a separate plastic bag and she added them to her and Lisa's packs as well as one roll into the boy's pile. The toothbrushes, toothpaste and deodorant were divided up and put into the different piles. Picturing again the boredom of floating on the open sea with nothing to do, she found an extra deck of cards and a notepad and pens. Estimating that there were enough supplies piled up to fill the backpacks, she decided to finish off her and Lisa's bags.

Mason and Mark came out of their rooms with clothes and settled onto the floor and started to fill their own bags. Emily was feeling good with the work and having some control over what might happen so she smiled at Mason when he looked her way.

"If there is anything you guys think we might have forgotten, let me know," she told him.

"I think this is all we'll need, Emily. It was a really good idea and even if nothing happens, we will be ready to go once we hit land."

"Thanks, Mason, but it was David's idea."

Mark smirked. "Yeah, good thing we have the Boy Scout to take care of us. We'd never make it without him," he said sarcastically as he stuffed instant noodles into his pack.

Emily gave him a look of disgust. "What is your problem, Mark? Why do you always have to be so nasty? David's done nothing but help our group. What have you done except for make snide comments and glower at everyone? Seriously, get over yourself!" she fired back at him.

He snarled at her, "You little…" but Mason jumped in before he could finish the sentence.

"Man, chill out! Lay off a bit. You have been snarly and you need to remember we're in this together."

Mark just stared at Mason with a flat expression until finally he nodded and muttered, "Together…right." And he went back to packing.

There was a tense silence as they went about their work until David came back down the stairs.

"Hey, good news! Tim says that the lifeboat he has comes with a weather shield. Sort of like a tent so we will have protection from the sun. He said it also has some survival supplies in it already so that will help. He's going to pack his own bag and will attach them all to the capsule himself. Even if nothing happens, this will help us be ready when we get to shore," he told everyone and settled down beside Mason to fill his own pack.

It wasn't long before they were done and the bags were ready. David took one last look around the cabin and asked, "Is that everything?" His eyes landed on the huge bottle of multi vitamins that was on the kitchen counter. He jumped up and grabbed it. He pulled the last of the Ziploc bags out of the now empty box and started to fill them with the pills. He left some in the bottle and handed out the rest. After they were packed away he handed out black garbage bags and everyone dropped their backpacks into them and tied them tightly. Emily finished Lisa's bag and handed it to Mason. The boys carried all the bags up on deck and Emily went in to see what Lisa was doing.

Lisa was lying on the bed staring up at the ceiling. "I packed your backpack up and it's on deck with the others," Emily told her curtly.

Lisa glanced at her and gave a faint smile. "Thank you, Emily. I'm sorry I didn't help. I have a huge headache."

Emily softened at the apology. "Do you want me to get you a Tylenol?" she asked.

"Maybe later. I just want to lie down and close my eyes but thanks. Emily - do you think we'll get home?"

Emily sighed and lay down next to her. "Yes. It's going to be brutal once we start going overland but I think we'll make it if we use our heads. I'm worried about what's happening at home though. What about you, are you worried about your family?"

Lisa didn't reply for a while. Emily didn't think she was going to answer when she finally started to speak.

"I don't think my mom will be doing very well. She's, well, let's just say high maintenance. Appearances mean a lot to her. She's not going to be very happy with no power or running water. I don't even know if my dad will be there. He spends a lot of time in the city so he might not of even been there when this all started." She started to giggle. "Sorry, just trying to picture my mother cooking food over a campfire in the backyard while wearing high heels!"

Emily laughed. "I'm sure she'll figure it out."

Lisa snorted. "Yeah, or find a big strong man to do it for her!"

Emily and Lisa stared up at the ceiling and thought about home until they both drifted off to sleep.

Chapter 9

Emily counted the days since her world had changed. Ten days had passed since they had sailed away from the burning city and four days since they had sailed through the cemetery of lifeboats. Tim had said that the lifeboats they had seen were old and out of date, probably coming from some poor country's frigate. He said that all modern lifeboats came with weather shields and supplies. That didn't help the sadness Emily felt when she thought of all those dead men dying so far from their homes and families. Sitting out on the deck in the bright sunshine, she glanced at the pile of black garbage bags beside the Lawless' lifeboat capsule. Tim said they were making great time and he thought it would only be another five or six days until they arrived at the Washington coast.

She tipped her head back and soaked up the warm sun. They had been lucky with the weather so far but Tim expected rain anytime. Looking over at Lisa, she shook her head at the bikini-wearing girl. She wished they were friends. Emily missed Alex so much and it would have made things easier if she and Lisa were closer. Lisa kept to herself, either sun tanning or lying in bed. She never joined them to play cards or the few board games that were aboard. Mark also kept to himself and seemed to brood more and more as the days passed. Mason helped Tim and seemed to really enjoy all he was learning about sailing. That left Emily and David to play cards, read the few books onboard and study the maps for the journey ahead. Time seemed to crawl and Emily just wanted to get to land and get moving.

The sun was slowly sinking into the horizon behind them and the breeze had cooled enough that Lisa shivered. She got up and grabbed her towel and headed down into the cabin. Dinner had been a simple dish of pasta with some canned ham in it. With nothing fresh on board, Emily was surprised at how much she craved fresh vegetables. She reminded herself that she was lucky and there were a lot of people who were probably starving right now, but she still thought a nice fresh tossed salad would be worth killing for.

"Well, maybe not quite yet, but maybe not that far in the future either," she thought to herself. With nothing else to do until bedtime, she stayed out on deck watching the waves, thinking about home and trying to guess where Alex and the others were right now.

When it was too dark to see anything, she got up and stretched her stiff legs. For one moment, she had the wild urge to dive off the side of the boat and swim as hard as she could. This had been the longest she had ever gone without swimming since she had started competing four years ago. Her body ached to move and stretch the way it was used to.

Mason was at the wheel when she headed towards the stairs and he waved her over to him. When she stepped up beside him, he put his arm around her and pulled her close. They were alone on the deck and Emily realized that this was probably the first time they had been alone together for more than a couple of minutes since it had all began. She still didn't know how to tell him that she didn't want to be his girlfriend anymore. It wasn't that she had hard feelings towards Mason, more that she had lost her feelings for him. What she did know was that she didn't want to cause any drama while they were stuck on the boat together.

Mason dipped his head down and started to kiss Emily's neck causing her to tense up. She tried to move away from him but he tightened his arm around her and held her close.

"Mason, please stop. This isn't the time or place for this," she told him gently.

He huffed out a breath of frustration. "Then when, Emily, once we are on land? At least here we have a comfy bed. Come on, don't worry so much. I have condoms. It'll be fine," he tried to convince her.

Emily was about to tell him that they wouldn't ever be together like that when his condom comment rocked her back. She shoved his arm off of her and turned to him. "Condoms? Where did you get condoms from?"

With a secretive grin he told her, "I grabbed some at that convenience store we first stopped at. I wanted to be prepared." He leaned in to try to kiss her again. She shoved him back and shook her head at him in disbelief.

"Are you telling me that after all we had seen that morning, all the death and destruction, all you really cared about was making sure you could get laid?!" Shaking her head at him, she backed away towards the stairs. "What is wrong with you?" Before he could reply, she thumped down the stairs and headed into the bedroom, passing Lisa who was sitting at the dinette painting her nails.

Lisa's eyes followed Emily to the bedroom and watched her shut the door. She glanced at Tim who was snoring on the couch and then looked towards the stairs. She finished her nails and waited a few minutes for them to dry, then quietly got up and went up the stairs.

Emily had thrown herself onto the bed and stared moodily up at the ceiling. She wasn't even mad at Mason. He was who he was and she had known that when she first started tutoring him. She was the one who had thought there was more to him. God, she felt like such an idiot. Did she really think that they had anything in common? She slammed her fists down onto the bed in self-reproach. All the time she spent with him and his jerk friends, the damage she had done to her and Alex's friendship and being stuck on this boat with them was all her fault.

After a few more minutes of mentally yelling at herself, she sat up and took a deep breath. She wasn't going to hide in this room. She was going to go and tell Mason how she felt and hope he didn't take it too badly. She got up and left the bedroom. Tim's soft snores drew her eyes to him, and she stopped briefly to throw a blanket over him. This distracted her enough that she didn't even stop to wonder where Lisa had gone. Standing at the bottom of the stairs, she took a deep fortifying breath and hoped Mason didn't flip out.

The sun was all the way down and it was dark on deck as she came up the stairs. She could just make out Mason's outline behind the wheel. Leaving the stairs and moving to the side let enough light from the cabin shine through the opening so she could clearly see that he wasn't alone. Mason and Lisa were lip locked and he had his hand up her shirt. Emily's mouth dropped open at the shocking sight. She had to stifle a laugh when the first thought that popped into her head was, "Thank God!" and she must have made a noise because Mason lifted his head and looked towards her. His eyes got huge at the sight of Emily standing there and he quickly removed his hand from Lisa's shirt and shoved her away from him.

"Emily! Emily, it's not what you think. I can explain!" he pleaded.

Emily had to try hard not to smile when she glanced at Lisa and saw her rubbing her bruised butt from where she had fallen and the scowl that she was directing at Mason.

"No, no, it's okay. Really! Carry on. Sorry to interrupt!"

She turned around and fled back down the stairs with her hand covering her mouth so she wouldn't burst out laughing. Emily took a few steps towards her room but stopped. She knew that Mason couldn't come after her because he had to stay on deck while Tim was asleep but she also had no desire to talk to Lisa who would be returning to their room at some point. So instead of going to the main bedroom, she went to David's room and knocked softly on his door.

David opened the door quickly but it was clear to Emily that he had been sleeping. His soft brown hair was rumpled and his eyes were blurry with sleep and confusion.

"Em...what's wrong?"

"Can I come in? I just need to lie low tonight."

David nodded and backed up so she could squeeze past him in the small and narrow room. The two bedrooms in the front of the boat followed the contour of the hull, making the rooms wide at the entrance and narrowing towards the bow. The beds mimicked the room, being wide near the door where the pillows were and narrowing towards the feet.

Emily pushed into the room and settled onto the unmade bed. David shut the door and turned to her with a question on his face. She had to cover her mouth to contain the laughter that wanted to spill out. David settled down beside her and she shifted to face him.

"Well, it's safe to say that Mason and I have broken up! I was going up on deck to break up with him and I was so worried he was going to make a scene or cause drama. Turns out he had his hands full...of Lisa! They were up there making out. This makes things so much better. Now he and Lisa can be together and I don't have to worry about him making things difficult. It's just really funny to me because I was so worried about hurting his feelings," she explained to him.

David shook his head. "You're not upset? I mean, about him cheating on you with Lisa?"

"Not at all, I was going to break up with him anyway. I've been an idiot all these months dating him. We really have nothing in common and him cheating on me just goes to show how different we are. Anyway, all I really feel is relief. Do you mind if I bunk in here with you tonight? I really don't want to deal with either of them until tomorrow."

"Yeah, of course, you take the bed and I'll take the floor." David stood up and grabbed a blanket.

Emily laughed, "David, don't be silly. We can share the bed. We've been camping together for years. Sleeping together in a bed is no different than that." She scooted over close to the wall and patted the space beside her on the bed.

David stood clutching the blanket in front of himself for a moment before giving his head a quick shake. "Yeah, you're right."

He settled into the bed with his back turned towards Emily. As he listened to her soft breathing, he wondered if he would ever have the courage to tell her how he felt.

** ** ** ** ** ** ** ** ** **

When Emily woke up the next morning, she was stretched out across the bed and David was gone. She stayed nestled in the warmth of the blankets and thought about what was to come that day. Dealing with Mason and Lisa wouldn't be fun but she was determined to keep things calm. She had no hard feelings toward either of them and if they were happy together it would only make the rest of their trip home easier. Stretching out, she decided there was no point in prolonging it so she got out of bed and slipped on her shoes. What she didn't expect was to come face to face with Mason the minute she opened the door. The intense expression on his face made her back up and he followed her into the room and shut the door behind him.

"Emily, you have to let me explain," he said before she could even open her mouth. "What you saw doesn't mean anything. I was frustrated because you keep putting me off. I just had a moment of weakness. Lisa threw herself at me and I got caught up. It didn't mean anything! I love you and we can put this behind us!"

Emily's mind was blank for a minute before anger flooded her. "Damn it! Now I have to break up with him anyway!" she thought.

"Mason, it's you that doesn't understand! I was coming up on deck to break up with you. You and Lisa would make a way better couple than us. I decided days ago that we shouldn't be together. We have nothing in common and we don't even think the same way about things. I was fooling myself these past few months. It's better this way. We just don't fit!" At his thunderous expression, she rushed on. "Please, Mason, you know that we don't make a very good couple! We need to work together to get home, but I can't be your girlfriend. Can we just be friends…please?" she begged him.

His face had gone blank. "Friends…you want to be friends."

Emily stepped forward and took his hand. "Mason, we don't need to fight or be angry. We can work together without tension. If I can manage to not be bitter about you and Lisa, you can be okay with this. Please, Mason, this boat isn't big enough for us to be at odds with each other and we still have a long way to go together to get home."

Mason studied her face and then pulled his hand away from her. "You're right, Emily, we don't make a good couple. At least Lisa puts out whenever I want it. I was getting tired of your little girl virgin issues anyway," he said before turning and walking out.

Emily sighed in frustration and shook her head in disbelief. What an asshole! How did she ever think he was something more?

"I'm going to have to talk to David," she thought. "It might be smarter to go our own way when we hit land."

She left the bedroom and went into the bathroom to wash her face and brush her teeth. The cabin was empty when she came out and she was grateful she didn't have to talk to anyone in her current state of mind. Emily grabbed a bottle of water and a granola bar out of the kitchen and carried it into the main bedroom that she had been sharing with Lisa. She was looking down when she entered the room so she didn't see Lisa sitting on the bed waiting for her.

It was the exasperated tone when Lisa muttered "Finally" that alerted her and she almost dropped her water bottle.

Emily couldn't muffle the groan at the sight of the girl. First Mason and now Lisa! Fine, better to get the whole thing over with and then they could all move on. She straightened her shoulders and faced Lisa with an expectant expression.

Lisa had her regular haughty look on her face but her eyes seemed to have a hard time meeting Emily's and when they did it seemed to her that there was something almost like shame in them.

Lisa took a deep breath and blurted "You need to let Mason go! You're not the right girlfriend for him. Last night wasn't the first time we've been together. We've been hooking up for longer than you guys have been dating. You need to let him go so we can be together!" she stated defiantly.

Emily studied Lisa in silence. Lisa seemed almost desperate. Emily thought about the nasty things Mason had said about Lisa putting out and she shook her head. She just couldn't understand how Lisa could let that jerk use her in that way. Her shoulders slumped and she sat down on the bed facing Lisa.

She tilted her head to the side and looked at Lisa with compassion. "Who lied to you? Who told you that you aren't worth more?" she asked softly.

"What the hell are you talking about!" Lisa stormed.

Emily held her hand up in a stopping gesture. "No, really, Lisa, I'm not being mean. I used to think that you were this shallow, selfish, empty girl but I've seen that there is more to you on this trip. I mean, think about it. You know you're gorgeous and I know you're smart or you wouldn't have had the grades to win this trip to Disney Land. I've seen you be thoughtful and funny too. So with all that going for you, why would you want that jerk to be your boyfriend when you deserve so much more?"

Lisa opened and closed her mouth half in anger and half in confusion. "I…you…if you just let him go, we can be together!" she finally said in desperation.

Emily shook her head, "You know that's not true, Lisa. If you've been "hooking up" since before we started dating then why weren't you guys a couple?" When Lisa didn't answer her, Emily went on. "I did break up with Mason. I was actually going to do it when I came upstairs last night and found you guys together. This morning he tried to get me to forgive him and stay his girlfriend. He told me that you didn't mean anything to him and when he saw that I wouldn't change my mind, he told me that at least he could get you to put out! I'm really not trying to be mean. I just want to understand why you would let him treat you like that. He's using you like…like…Kleenex! Every time he needs one, he uses it and then throws it away. You're worth more than that!"

Lisa wouldn't look at Emily. She stared at her hands folded into her lap but Emily could see the tears dripping off of her chin. She tried to find the words to reach the girl.

"Everything is different now. It doesn't matter who was popular in high school. All that matters now is survival. Taking care of each other and getting home. If you really think that Mason is the guy for you then go for it, but make sure that he treats you right! You need to be able to count on him. I couldn't and I deserve better, so do you," she finished and slid off the bed. Emily left the room and Lisa to think over everything she had said. All she felt was sadness for a girl who could have it all but didn't believe that she deserved it.

Chapter 10

Lisa laid in her canopied princess bed and looked around at her pink bedroom. The elegant white with gold accent furniture gleamed in the soft morning light. She loved her room and everything in it. From her walk in closet full of beautiful clothes to the spa-like ensuite bathroom that was hers alone, but nothing in the room could make her feel better this morning. She had caught a flu bug somewhere and had been up all night throwing up. Her hair was matted from sweat and her skin felt and looked greasy. Her normally tan skin had a greenish cast to it and she had deep dark bags under her eyes.

Lisa slowly rolled out of bed and staggered to the door. She needed to go to the kitchen for some water and crackers to soothe her aching stomach. She made her way down the hall to the stairs and clutched the gleaming banister to steady herself on the way down. Looking longingly at the stylish furnishing in the front sitting room, Lisa wanted to rest on one of the elegant Queen Anne chairs but knew her mother would shriek if she caught her on it. The front room was only for guests. Her head swam with dizziness and she had to take deep breaths to control the nausea that threatened to erupt. Getting sick on the imported African hardwood floor was not an option in this house.

She finally managed to make it into the kitchen and had to lay her head against the cool marble countertop before she could go any further. She had just closed her eyes briefly when her mother's shrill voice cut through the air.

"Lisa, just what do you think you are doing!"

Lisa raised her head and looked at her mother through blurry eyes. As usual, she looked like she had just stepped out of a fashion magazine. Every hair was in place and her dress had not a wrinkle in it. The only thing not beautiful about her mother was the ugly scowl that was on her face as she looked in disgust at her daughter.

"I'm sick, Mom. I need some water and crackers and medicine," she told her in a weary voice.

"Well, I can see that! You look absolutely haggard. You shouldn't have come downstairs without cleaning yourself up first. What if we had company! Being sick is no excuse for looking like that. Now go to your room and I will bring you what you need and I don't want to see you out of that room again until you look presentable, young lady. Really!" Her mother lectured with no compassion.

Lisa slowly made her way back to her room wondering what it would be like to feel her mother's cool hand on her forehead like she had read in books. Her parents had always given her anything she wanted - clothes, trips to the spa and even a new little convertible car for her sixteenth birthday, but never affection. Image was everything to them, and as long as she looked the part of their little princess, they were happy. Lisa remembered when she was little and she wanted to join girl guides with her friends but her mother refused because she said the uniforms were too ugly. It was the same with school and sports. Soccer was a no because she would get too sweaty and good grades were a must but not extra credit projects because her mother said boys didn't like brainy girls.

Collapsing onto her bed with the room spinning around her she wished briefly for different parents, ones that only cared about her happiness and not just how she looked to the outside world. Her mother came into her room carrying a breakfast tray with her sickroom supplies and placed it beside the bed. She studied her daughter with a frown.

"You will need to get past this quickly, Lisa. You have a football game tomorrow night and as Captain of the cheer squad you need to be there. Besides that, I'm sure Mason will miss you if you aren't there."

Lisa groaned, "Mom, Mason isn't my boyfriend. I think he's going to ask out Emily, his tutor."

Her mother waved her hand dismissively. "Don't be ridiculous! He's the quarterback and you are the captain of the cheerleaders. You two are supposed to be a couple.

You just need to be more persuasive. What reason would Mason have for dating this brainy little farm girl? Unless…she's giving him something that he really wants!" She raised her eyebrows at Lisa until she looked up from the cracker she was nibbling. "Lisa, there are certain things that a woman has to sacrifice to get what she wants…Keep that in mind. I expect you to be with Mason on stage for prom. You two will make a beautiful Queen and King. Don't let me down. Now, get some rest and then clean yourself up. I will see you at breakfast tomorrow." With a sharp nod of her head, she turned on her stylish high heels, and left her daughter's room.

** ** ** ** ** ** ** ** ** **

Lisa sat on the bed with her arms wrapped around her drawn up knees. Tears streamed down her cheeks as Emily's words rang in her head. Lisa found herself reevaluating her life and the decisions she had made. She thought about her beautiful, perfect mother and the things she expected from her daughter. She remembered how her mother had taken her to the doctor for birth control and how she had reminded Lisa to do whatever it took to get Mason. She felt shame wash over her at the memory of the first time she had sex with Mason and the heart-stopping humiliation of seeing him walk the hallways two days later holding Emily's hand. The sharp, biting remarks from her mother encouraged her to make herself available to Mason whenever he wanted her that way. Lisa saw all of that in a new light thanks to Emily's words. She had let him use her and she was a fool. At that moment, Lisa hated her mother with every fiber of her damaged soul.

Rage filled her. Rage against her mother for not caring about her happiness, only her image. Rage against Mason for the casual way he used and discarded her. Never again would she allow others to dictate her actions. Emily was right, she was worth more and she would never settle for less again.

Lisa stayed in the bedroom for the rest of the day thinking about the person she wanted to be and the choices she would have to make to survive in this new world. She knew that the others thought that she was oblivious to the situation they were in but she had heard every word of the grim future that they had painted. Things would be different when they got home. High school was over and the main things in life would be finding or growing food. She would not be her mother. She would never again sell herself to some man to provide for her. Lisa vowed to make amends to Emily and David and beg them to teach and help her to learn the things she would need to provide for herself. Spa treatments and manicures would no longer be in her future. She looked over to the nightstand where there was a bottle of pink nail polish sitting. She reached over and picked it up. Slowly turning it in her hand she said goodbye to Princess Lisa and leaned over and dropped it into the waste can beside the bed.

No one on deck knew of the major shift going on under their feet. Emily and David sat talking quietly at the front of the boat. They were making plans to go their own way once they got to land. They did this while Mason kept stealing looks at them. Mark sat beside Mason with an amused smirk on his face. He was enjoying the tension coming off of Mason. It wasn't very often that his golden-boy best friend got shot down and it was a nice change for Mark.

Mark was one of five boys in his family. He was the second youngest and was often ignored. His older brothers were all big like him, and until he hit his growth spurt, had often bullied him. He had to learn to fight back and took out his frustrations on his only little brother. His mother was always tired and never seemed to have time for all of her children. She worked long hours and the boys were often left to fend for themselves. Mark's father was also absent most of the time. He worked on oil rigs up in the northern part of Alberta and stayed in camps. When he did come home, he only wanted quiet in the house so he could watch sports on TV and drink huge amounts of beer. Mark had intimate knowledge of the back of his father's hand from getting between him and the TV.

Never first place with five other boys at home to compete against; Mark was often filled with rage and bitterness. He was smart enough to know that he didn't have the looks or the right clothing to be popular at school so he joined the football team in junior high and let his size take out anyone in front of him. Even back then he saw how Mason shone and how everyone wanted to be near him. It had been easy to get in with the star of the team and he stuck like glue all the way into high school, earning himself a spot in the popular crowd by association. But once again Mark was not first. Always in Mason's shadow, he had learned to temper down his bitterness.

Now was his chance. Good looks and sports talent wouldn't be enough in this new world and Mark knew that with his size and brutal nature he would finally have his spot as number one. He wasn't ready to make his move yet but it would be soon and in the meantime he enjoyed watching Mason stew in defeat.

Tim stood at the wheel and watched all of this unfold on his boat. He didn't regret taking all these kids along but he would be happy when they landed and he would go his own way. He had put his time in and had no desire to relive high school politics. He really liked Emily and David and he suspected that they were planning on going their own way. It would probably make the difference between surviving or not. From all that he had observed so far, Lisa would be a dead weight that they would have to carry and Mark was volatile enough that there would be a power struggle somewhere down the road. Mason could go either way. He could man up and be the team player that they needed or stay petulant now that he was no longer the star of the show.

"Hard to tell what will happen." he mused. "I hope they make out okay, but I'm glad I won't be around to deal with it."

Tim breathed in the salty tang of the sea air and tilted his head up to the sun. They had been incredibly lucky with the weather so far but he knew it wouldn't last. The closer they got to home, the greater the chances of a storm.

Springtime in Washington wasn't known for its sunny skies. Scanning the ocean ahead of him, he also knew that they would start to see more stranded vessels soon. Four or five days to go and he'd be headed to his family cabin. He sent a prayer up that his family would be there waiting for him.

Chapter 11

Dinner that night was a silent and tense meal of rice and canned tuna. David and Emily sat at the table and ate quietly. Mark ate his meal standing at the counter and Emily kept her eyes away from him as he shoveled the food in to his mouth. Mason took two bowls up on deck for himself and Tim and Lisa hid in the bedroom. Emily was worried about the girl and when she finished her meal, she was going to go and check on her.

Emily stood and gathered her and David's bowl to put them in the sink when Mason came back down and brushed past her. He went straight to the bedroom door and knocked briefly before entering and closing it behind him. As Emily turned to go back to the table, she met Mark's eyes and wasn't surprised to see the amusement in them. She felt a small shiver go down her spine and quickly looked away. There was something sinister about him and Emily was counting the days until she could get away from him.

She helped David spread the maps across the table and they bent their heads to study them together. They were trying to determine the best route to take through Washington State. They wanted to avoid the major population centers but they also had mountains that they would have to get around or over. Emily cursed for the thousandth time the lack of technology. A few minutes on Google Earth and they would have a much better understanding of the terrain and populations of all the towns listed on the map.

The sound of a door being thrown open and slamming into a wall was like a gunshot in the small cabin. All eyes turned towards Mason as he stormed out of Lisa's room. His face was furious and as his gaze found Emily, he let out a snarl. He came to a stop in front of the table and stared at her in anger. She waited for him to start yelling but after a minute of staring at her, the anger in his eyes seemed to slide away and before he whirled away to stomp up the stairs, she thought he was going to cry. The look in his eyes said he was lost.

Mark's head swiveled from the empty stairs to Lisa's now closed bedroom door and then back to the stairs before turning to look at Emily. There was a beat of silence before he let out a sharp, hard bark of laughter. He slapped his leg and laughed some more.

Emily looked to David in confusion but he just shrugged his shoulders. He was just as mystified by Mark's reaction as she was. Emily looked to the closed bedroom door and sighed. Lisa must have taken her words to heart and turned Mason down. For a brief moment, she felt sorry for Mason. In one day, he had lost his girlfriend, lost his mistress, for lack of a better word, and now his best friend was clearly enjoying his misery. She shook her head. Mason had made the choices that brought him to these circumstances and he would have to live with them.

Mark had stopped laughing and was looking at Lisa's door intensely before he turned and followed Mason up the stairs. Emily looked at the door too and was trying to decide if she should go and talk to the girl when David squeezed her arm and shook his head.

"Just leave her. She will come out when she is ready."

"I know. I just hate all this drama. It's so...so...high school!" she laughed. "This crap is the last thing we should be worrying about, right?"

"Yeah, I know. It will straighten itself out. A few more days and we will be too busy trying to stay alive to worry about anything else." He went back to the map for a minute and then let out a laugh.

"What?" Emily asked.

"Just thinking this would make a really good reality TV show. It's the end of the world as we know it so we put a bunch of kids from different social groups on a sailboat in the middle of the ocean and watch them tear each other apart! I bet that would make prime time!"

Emily laughed at his announcer voice. "I never was much of a reality show girl but I know what you mean. I can't help but think of all the things we will never have again. Do you know how many times I've reached for my phone to text Alex? It just feels like so much is gone and at the same time none of it really matters. TV, cell phones, internet, it made things easier but we can live without all that stuff. It's other things that I'll really miss, like my swim team, for one. This is the longest I've gone without swimming in four years, all that work and training and now…no Olympics. I'll never have a shot at winning a gold medal. It's going to be really hard to let that dream go," she said quietly.

David gently squeezed her hand. "I'm sorry, Em."

She gave him a small smile and turned back to studying the map.

Up on deck, Mason stood at the bow and watched the empty ocean slide by. He was miserable, and the worst part was he knew it was his own fault. He had ruined everything, and he didn't know what to do to fix it. When Emily had first started to tutor him, he had used his charm on her figuring she would be easily swayed by it. The more he flirted with her, the more she looked at him with contempt. There was something so fresh and real about her that he found himself looking forward to every conversation. When he let go of the fake charm and just talked to her she warmed up to him. They started to talk on the phone and their conversations grew longer and longer. He found himself confiding in her. Things he hadn't told anyone or hardly even admitted to himself, he told her. There was just something so attractive about Emily and the way she wasn't impressed by his status in school. She was interested in him, Mason the person not Mason the quarterback. When they were alone together he felt like he could be himself and she made him feel like he was a good person.

Mason knew what he was doing with Lisa was wrong but she made it so easy. He had thought it would be the one time but even after he had started dating Emily, Lisa had made it clear that she would be with him in that way. He knew deep down that Lisa wanted to be his girlfriend and she was only having sex with him to try and persuade him. He knew he was using her but he had just pushed the guilt down. He thought about Lisa's tear-filled face and the sadness in her eyes when she had told him she was done being used and that she deserved better. He thought about Emily's heartfelt plea for them to be friends when she had every right to be furious with him for what he had done. But what really brought it home was how he had felt sitting alone in the golf cart after he had left Emily in the middle of the street during the gunfire. He had felt like a selfish coward and he realized that that was exactly what he was.

Lost and alone, he thought back on the past few years of his life. Always being compared to his older brother had driven him to be a better football player and more popular in school. He had been so absorbed in being better than his brother that he stopped caring about anyone but himself. Mason didn't want to be that person. He wanted to be the guy that would be there for his friends and put others first. He knew that if he couldn't find a way to make amends and change his ways, he would end up all alone in this new world.

Standing at the rail and looking out at the empty ocean with the sun setting behind him, Mason had no way of knowing that Lisa had come to the same conclusions hours earlier. He just knew that everything he thought about himself and others had just shifted and it would take a lot of hard work to stay there.

Mason heard Mark's lumbering footsteps before his friend joined him at the rail. His friend just stood beside him for a minute before speaking.

"Tough day for you, bro. Shot down from all sides!" he exclaimed.

Without even looking at Mark, Mason muttered, "It's my own fault."

"Whoa! Looks like little goody goody Emily's influenced more than just Lisa," he laughed.

Mason turned to look at him with a frown. "It was wrong. I was wrong. I treated them both badly."

Mark laughed, "It's only wrong if you get caught, buddy, and you are so busted!"

Mason looked away and rubbed his hands over his face. He tried to remember why he was friends with Mark and couldn't come up with anything. They played football together and hung out in the halls and at parties but Mason couldn't think of anything that really connected them. It was just one more way he had been selfish and self-involved. He turned back to Mark and tried to do better.

"We haven't really talked about what's going on. Are you worried about your family?"

"As if! The last thing I would want to do right now is have to fight my brothers for food. Trust me, they're fine. Besides, I'm sure my mom is just happy she has one less mouth to feed," Mark said sarcastically.

Mason studied his face and realized that he meant what he said. "Wow, that's cold."

Mark shrugged, "That's life. Don't sweat it. I'm not." He grinned in a not nice way. "So are you and Lisa done? Is she back on the market?"

Mason shook his head. There really wasn't anything to this guy. "Yeah, good luck with that," and he turned to look back out at the passing ocean so he didn't see the smirk on Mark's face.

"Well, it's a brand new world, anything could happen." he said in a bland tone and turned and walked away.

Mason thought about Mark's words. It was a brand new world and he was determined to be a brand new person in it. Tim called out to him from the wheel and he went to join him there. There was still a lot to learn about sailing and he would do his best to help get them all home.

Mark came down into the cabin in time to see Emily and David disappear into David's room and shut the door. He gave a smirk and laughed to himself that Emily hadn't taken very long to move on. He looked to Lisa's closed bedroom door and then back up the stairs. After a moment, Mark settled down onto the couch and closed his eyes. It wasn't long before he heard Mason come down and go into the other bedroom for the night. Tim would stay up on deck at the wheel for most of the night. He had told them that as they got closer to land they would run into more and more stranded vessels and they would have to keep a close watch so they didn't run into any of them. Tim had said that this would be the last night he would keep sailing in the dark. They would anchor at night starting tomorrow.

It was an hour later and Mark hadn't heard any noises coming from the bedrooms in a while. He eased himself off the couch and quietly made his way to just beside the stairs to the deck. Peeking around the corner, he could just see the edge of Tim's arm at the wheel. He backed up further into the cabin and crossed to the other side of it. It was only a few steps before he was standing at Lisa's bedroom door. He leaned his forehead against the door and closed his eyes, listening for any sounds from within. Standing there he let his mind go back to all the times she had put him down and used her nasty sarcasm to wound him. He let the cold rage fill him and he took a deep breath before opening the door.

The soft light of the bedside lamp shone over Lisa who was sitting back against the pillows on the bed. She was reading a book and glanced up when her door opened. It took a moment before her brain processed that it was Mark in her room and not Emily. Shutting the book with a snap, she scowled at him.

"What do you want?" she demanded. A shot of fear went through her when he didn't answer her but continued to stare at her. "Mark, what do you want?" she asked again.

He stayed where he was with his back to the door and cocked his head to one side. "I thought we should talk about what's going to happen in the future. You understand that everything is different now, don't you?" he asked softly.

Lisa frowned in confusion. Mark had never really spoken to her about anything and he hadn't really seemed all that concerned with the current crisis. She wondered if he was starting to worry about his future too.

"Yes, I know that things are different and I know how hard life is going to get when we get off this boat."

He nodded his head. "Good. I wanted to make sure you understand that only the strong will survive and that nothing will be free from now on. In this new world, everyone will have to be useful or have something to barter if they want to live." He paused and looked at her thoughtfully. "It seems to me that you won't be very useful. You're the kind of girl who will have to be taken care of and now that you dumped Mason, there's no one who will do that."

Anger filled Lisa. As if she needed this jerk to tell her how inadequate she was to deal with and survive what was coming. She had spent all day coming to terms with that very thing.

She snarled at him, "Get out!"

Mark didn't seem to hear her as he took a step towards the bed. "I don't want you to worry. You have something that I value. I'll take care of you and make sure you live as long as you take care of me."

He took another step towards the bed.

Lisa pushed herself further up against the pillows. She was angry and scared at the same time. There was a blank glaze to Mark's eyes. "I don't need your help. I can take care of myself. Just get out of my room," she said the last with a slight tremble in her voice.

He took one more step and he was up against the bed. "The people with power will rule now. If you want to live, you'll need to make them happy."

He reached behind his back and pulled out a small handgun. He held it in his hands and stared down at it almost lovingly. At Lisa's gasp, his head whipped up and their eyes met. The blank glazed look was gone and in its place was cold as ice determination.

"This gives me the power now and you will make yourself useful to me or you won't be making it off this boat. You will want to be quiet now or things will go very badly," he told her in a flat, hard voice.

Lisa stared wide-eyed at the gun and felt tears trickle down her face. When Mark reached out and grabbed her ankle in a vise-tight grip and dragged her down the length of the bed, it was only a small whimper that escaped her throat, not nearly loud enough for anyone on the boat to hear.

Chapter 12

When Emily woke the next morning, she laid still and listened to David's quiet breathing. She was so grateful to have him onboard with her. The ache in her lower back told her that sleeping in the cramped single bed with him was over. She needed to make peace with Lisa and that thought reminded her that they were almost to land. A few more days and they would start the final journey towards home. She was scared and excited all at the same time. Other than the high school drama, things had been so easy so far. Once they stepped off this boat, all that would change. She quietly left the bed and stepped out into the main cabin. There was no one in the room so she went to the bathroom and got cleaned up and brushed her teeth. There was no longer enough water for showers so she had a quick wash with a cloth and braided her hair back. When she came out, the cabin was still empty so she decided to make breakfast. They still had plenty of propane for the small stove so she dragged out the biggest pot and started making oatmeal. Emily added raisins and dried cranberries to sweeten it and left it on the stove to boil.

With only a few days left, she decided that today would be a good day to wash all of the dirty clothes. They wouldn't be able to do much with them once they were walking. She went to her and Lisa's door and knocked softly before opening it and going in. Emily didn't even look at the bed but went straight to the pile of dirty clothes she and Lisa had been throwing in the corner. Gathering them up in her arms she turned to go back out when her eyes landed on the bed and she froze with surprise.

Sprawled across the bed with a sheet pulled over him was Mark. Even in sleep his face hadn't softened, it still had a scowl on it. Emily glanced around but Lisa wasn't in the room so she quickly left and softly closed the door behind her. She dumped the dirty laundry on one end of the couch and gave the oatmeal a quick stir. She turned the heat down on it and went over to the panel that had the gauges that showed the boats holding tanks levels. There was a quarter tank of fresh water left. They still had plenty of water bottles and jugs left so she figured it would be okay to wash the clothes as long as she used the water sparingly.

Emily went to the stairs and looked up to see who was at the wheel. Mason was standing behind it and looking ahead with a frown on his face. She pulled back and thought for a minute. Yesterday had been full of tension and she didn't want today to be a repeat. So she filled a bowl with the steaming oatmeal and grabbed a spoon. Carefully carrying it up the stairs she brought it to Mason and hoped he would take it as a peace offering.

He studied her face as she held the bowl out to him and then he reached out and took it with a small smile. "Can you take the wheel for a minute while I eat?" he asked. "Just hold it steady."

Emily stepped up to the wheel and took Mason's place while he took a seat close to her. They didn't speak for a while and Mason made short work of his breakfast. When he was done, he stared into his empty bowl.

"Thanks, Emily, this was really good. You should make a big pot of this before we leave the boat and take it with us. It would be easy to warm it up and it's great carb and fiber-loaded food for when we are walking a lot."

Emily was surprised at his comment. Mason hadn't really talked about preparations for the long walk ahead and his comment was a really good idea.

"That's a great idea, Mason. Good thinking!" She looked at him for a minute and then asked, "Are you okay?"

His head came up and his face showed confusion. "How can you be so nice to me after what I did to you?" he asked her in awe.

She shook her head. "You made a mistake, Mason. I know you are a good person but you struggle with it. Everybody makes mistakes. We're teenagers; we are supposed to make mistakes! Besides, this isn't really a good time to be fighting with each other. You know the whole end of the world thing? We really need to work together, especially in a few days when we hit land," she said with a laugh.

Mason looked out to sea and was quiet for a minute. When he turned back to face her, she saw such sadness on his face that she reached out her hand and grabbed his.

His voice was choked when he said, "God, I'm so sorry Emily. You didn't deserve to be treated the way I treated you. Please forgive me?"

"Oh, Mason, of course I forgive you! Listen, listen to me. This is not an excuse for what you did but I understand some of the reasons for why you act this way. I know how much pressure you get from your dad to live up to your brother's accomplishments. I know how hard he makes it for you to be the cool popular sports star. But your brother is a jerk! Just because he has talent with a football he thinks he can treat people like dirt. I mean, how many girls does the guy use and discard on a weekly basis? And the way he's always bragging about his conquests and putting you down whenever he's home. You have told me how much you don't like him so tell me why would you want to live up to that? If you really want to be better than your brother then be better than him. You've shown me the good person inside of you now you need to show the rest of the world." She wasn't surprised to see the tears in Mason's eyes and when his met hers, she finished. "Who you really need to show that to is Lisa."

He rubbed his eyes, took a deep breath and nodded. "She's over there at the bow. When Tim woke me up to change out with him she was already sitting out here. She hasn't moved in a couple of hours. I think I really hurt her, Emily. I don't know if an apology is going to be enough to fix this."

Emily left the wheel to Mason and moved to the side to get a better view of where Lisa was sitting. The girl had her knees pulled up to her chest and her arms wrapped tight around them. With a frown she turned back to Mason. "I went into our room this morning to get some clothes and Mark was sleeping in our bed. I think he was being a jerk and didn't want to take his turn on the couch.

He probably figured with me in David's room he should get to share the bed with her. No wonder she came out here."

Mason looked away from her and asked, "I know it's none of my business now but are you and David together?"

"What? No! Mason, I told you this before. David is one of my best friends. I just needed some space from you and Lisa so I stayed in his room. This really isn't the time to be playing musical boyfriends. Anyway, I think I'll get Lisa a bowl of oatmeal and try to talk to her but you need to as well. We need to fix this mess before we hit land. There will be enough to worry about then without us fighting with each other."

"You're a really good person, Emily. I wish things had turned out differently," Mason told her.

She gave him a sad smile and squeezed his arm before taking his empty bowl and going down to get Lisa some breakfast. She filled another bowl and said good morning to a sleepy David when he came out of the bathroom. Mark had still not come out of the main bedroom and she knew Tim would sleep for hours after staying up at the wheel all night. She handed the filled bowl to David and made another one to take up to Lisa. She considered eating it herself before taking one up to Lisa but the image of her sitting at the bow looking so alone made Emily push the thought aside. Grabbing another spoon, she carried the bowl up on deck and carefully made her way to the front of the boat where Lisa was sitting in a tight ball.

Lisa didn't seem to register Emily coming up beside her but when she kneeled down, the girl jerked away like she was going to be hit. The eyes that met Emily's were huge and had a sheen of tears on them. Taken aback by her reaction, Emily frowned in confusion.

"Oh Lisa, it's okay. I just brought you some breakfast!" she said compassionately.

Lisa took a deep breath and seemed to relax slightly. "You brought me breakfast?" she said, looking down at the bowl that Emily held out to her. When she looked back up into Emily's eyes, the tears started to trickle down her face. In a choked up voice she said, "After everything I've done to you, you brought me breakfast?" Lisa broke down into sobs. Her shoulders shook as she gasped out, "I'm sorry. I'm so sorry! I'm a horrible person and you are so nice. I'm sorry!"

Emily set the bowl down on the deck and wrapped the crying girl in her arms. She made soothing noises and rubbed her trembling back. It took a while but eventually Lisa's sobs quieted and she pulled back from Emily.

With red puffy eyes and a dripping nose, Lisa took a shuddering breath. "How can you be so nice? Why don't you hate me?"

Emily looked out at the waves while she considered Lisa's question. Finally, she turned back and tried to explain.

"We weren't friends. You obviously wanted to be with Mason before we started to date and I know you didn't sleep with him to hurt me." At Lisa's confused expression, Emily changed tact. "Alex is my best friend and has been for years. When I started dating Mason, I betrayed her by dropping her from my life. I dumped her for a guy. What I did to Alex was way worse than what you did to me, and Alex forgave me. She yelled at me first but she forgave me. So how can I not forgive you? Besides, you hurt someone else way more than you hurt me," Emily said sadly.

Lisa cast her eyes down in shame and whispered, "Me."

Emily put her hand on Lisa's shoulder. "You are going to have to forgive yourself. And then there's Mason." At that, Lisa scowled in his direction. "What he did was pretty crappy and I'm not going to make excuses for him but I talked to him this morning and he's feeling pretty awful. Strange as this may sound, I think he really gets what he did and wants to make amends." Emily picked up the now cool bowl of oatmeal and held it out to Lisa. "You should really eat this. The last thing you need right now is another round of sea sickness. Not eating and being tired can start that up again."

Lisa took the bowl and ate a spoonful. "Emily, I just want to say thank you. Even though we weren't friends before, you have treated me like one - so thanks."

Emily bumped shoulders with her and said, "Hey, we're outnumbered! Us girls need to stick together." Emily laughed. "Did you even get any sleep last night? I went in to our room this morning to get our dirty clothes to wash and saw Mark snoring away in our bed. Did the jerk decide he didn't want to sleep on the couch? Just because I stayed in David's room doesn't mean he gets to kick you out of there!" Emily said hotly.

Lisa looked away but not before Emily saw dark shadows come into her eyes. "Yeah...he wanted the bed," Lisa mumbled.

Emily knew what a bully Mark could be and shook her head. "Well, don't worry about it. It won't happen again. I'll be staying with you in there now that we've worked stuff out and I plan on giving him a piece of my mind!"

Lisa's head whipped around and she grabbed Emily's arm. "No! Don't do that. It's fine. It's not worth the fight. Just stay away from him. He will be trading with David tonight so it won't be a problem," she said almost desperately.

Emily frowned but nodded. She knew that Mark gave her the creeps and Lisa must feel that way too. Lisa was right. It wasn't worth getting into an argument with the guy.

"Okay, you're right but that guy is a major ass...you know what! Anyway, I'm going to go down and grab something to eat and then wash out our clothes." With that, she stood up to go.

Lisa looked up at her and shaded her eyes against the morning sun. "I'll do the next laundry day if you don't mind doing today's. I just want to stay up here and do some thinking."

"No problem, but I'm definitely holding you to that!" she promised. Emily went back down to the cabin, flashing Mason a quick smile as she passed. She had no idea that Lisa was desperately trying to avoid being in the cabin with Mark.

David was washing the breakfast dishes at the small sink and she asked him about his dirty clothes. She figured if she was going to do a wash she might as well do them all. Tim was still sleeping so his and Mason's clothes would have to wait until later. As far as she was concerned, Mark could do his own. The guy hadn't done any work on the boat so she had no problem letting him fend for himself. She ate a quick bowl of oatmeal while David gathered up his clothes and slipped her empty dish into the wash water. Adding David's clothes to the pile, she hauled it all to the bathroom.

Tim had a large plastic bucket that she filled with hot water and soap. Setting it in the shower/bath tub in the bathroom, Emily plunged each piece of clothing in and swished it around and tried to rub the fabric together to clean it. It wasn't the best way to clean clothes but it was all she could think of under the circumstances. After she had wrung the soapy water out of each item, she tossed it to the side. Once everything had been through the soapy water, she emptied out the bucket and filled it back up with clean water. Repeating the whole process with each article of clothing took forever and she had to stand up and stretch her aching back often. Emily let her mind wander while she worked and she flashed back on how much she used to complain when she had to do the laundry at home. Laughing at herself, she could only wish for the easy washing machine and dryer at home. She started to think about home and wondered if the generator they had on the farm still worked or if it was just as fried as everything else. That made her think of different ways they could get electricity and she made a mental note to ask David about a larger version of a science fair project they had done a few years ago in school. It was a simple windmill that they had set up to charge a battery. If they could make a large scale one it could maybe run a few things to make life easier. She was sure her dad had already thought about all these things but she wanted to think of the future and what they could do not just what they had lost.

It took over an hour to finish the job and her hands were just as sore as her back from wringing all the clothes out. She dumped the rinse water out and shoved all the wet clothes into the bucket. It was really heavy but she carried it out of the bathroom and into the cabin where she collided with Mark as he came stumbling out of the main bedroom. She dropped the bucket and clean, wet clothes fell out onto the floor with a wet splat. Groaning in frustration, she kneeled down to scoop them back up. Mark didn't even acknowledge her. He just walked past, stepping on some clothes as he went.

"Hey, don't mind me. I just spent over an hour working on getting these clean," she snapped sarcastically at him.

Mark spun around and scowled at her. "Watch your mouth, little girl!" and took a menacing step towards her.

Emily leaned back away from him and felt her back collide with a pair of legs. Looking up she saw that David was standing behind her glaring at Mark. The bully looked from David to Emily and gave his trademark smirk before turning and going into the bathroom and slamming the door.

Emily let out the breath she didn't even know she had been holding and reached down to gather up more of the fallen clothes. David squatted down and helped her then picked up the bucket and carried it up on to the deck for her. He set it down near the rail and Emily started to drape the clothes over it. She used the clothespins that she had found under the sink to secure them so they wouldn't blow away.

David stepped up to Mason at the wheel and quietly talked to him about Mark.

"What's up with your buddy? He gets nastier every day. He just about took Emily's head off down there and he was sleeping in Lisa's room last night. I know he likes to play the big mean bully, but this boat's a little small to have to deal with that," David told him with concern.

Mason looked down the stairs but he couldn't see far into the cabin. Turning to David, he shook his head.

"I don't know what's going on with him. I tried to talk to him last night but he just brushed me off. I'll talk to him later and see if he'll lay off." Mason looked at David thoughtfully. "Truth is though, I don't know if he'll even listen to me. I'm realizing I don't really even know the guy." He looked away and sighed before continuing. "I uh, just wanted to, um, say I'm sorry for being such a dick to you before. I've made some mistakes and I'm trying to…uh…be better," he stammered, his face turning red.

David studied the football player before responding. "Yeah, you definitely were a dick. But Emily saw something good in you or she wouldn't have dated you and I trust her, so let's just leave it in the past and work together to get home."

Mason nodded and David turned away to help Emily finish hanging the wet clothes. Lisa was still sitting at the front of the boat and her expression said she was far away in her thoughts. Once all the laundry was hung, the boat looked like a floating clothesline but it was the fastest way to get everything dry. No one wanted to deal with Mark so they all stayed up on deck and enjoyed the sun. They had been very lucky with the weather and had only suffered from mild rain a few times. Emily hoped it would last until they made it to shore. She didn't want to think about how it would feel to be trapped in the cabin during a storm.

Chapter 13

They had been up on deck for hours and Emily's stomach was growling enough that she knew it was past lunch. A lot of the lighter clothes like tee-shirts and socks and underwear were dry and they had unpinned them and folded them up. The heavier jeans and cargo pants were still damp but in the bright sun and warm wind it wouldn't take much longer until they were dry as well.

Emily was about to ask David if he would go down into the cabin and help her make some lunch when they heard a bellow from below. They looked at each other in confusion before taking a step towards the stairs. Lisa had bolted straight up at the first shout and now she scrambled to her feet. She grabbed Emily's arm to stop her and frantically shook her head. She was about to ask her why she looked so terrified when she heard Tim cursing as he stomped up the stairs on to the deck. He looked furious and zeroed right in on Mason.

"You need to get control of your sidekick down there. He's drunk! He drank my only bottle of Crown Royal and he's spouting off a bunch of bullshit!" he halfway yelled at Mason.

Mason looked past Tim and frowned when Mark came up the stairs with an almost empty bottle of whiskey clutched in his meaty hand. Mark stumbled on the last step and fell to one knee. Tim had turned around and scowled down at him.

"Get back downstairs, you idiot! You're so drunk you'll end up overboard," he said with disgust.

Mark lifted his head and met Tim's eyes. With a slurred voice, he muttered, "Fuck you."

Tim went still. The anger left his face and he stared down at Mark with contempt. He shook his head and looked away. When he turned back, Mark had gotten to his feet.

"Listen, kid. This is a big adjustment for all of us but getting trashed is not going to help you and insulting me is really not going to help you. Try to remember that I'm doing you a favor here and this is my boat so show a little respect." He started to turn away when Mark started to laugh.

"Thanks for the favor asshole but I don't think I'll need your help anymore," Mark spat out and pulled the gun out from under his shirt and pointed it at him.

Everyone froze and time seemed to slow. A click sounded in Emily's mind as she flashed back to the empty box of bullets beside the dead convenience store clerk. At the same time, David stepped in front of her so that he was between her and Mark. Mason threw his hands out in a "stop" motion and Tim just managed to croak out a single word, "Don't" before Mark squeezed the trigger.

It was as if Mark had shot them all. They all flew back away from him. Tim flew back against the rail and blood blossomed on his chest before he flipped back and disappeared over the rail into the ocean. Mason fell back onto his butt in shocked disbelief. David shoved Emily hard and they fell together onto the deck in a heap with him covering her. The only one who didn't move away from Mark was Lisa.

Emily watched in shock as Lisa took three quick steps towards Mark, dipped down to the deck and came up with the long handled paddle that had been resting in its brackets against the outer cabin wall. Two more steps and she lifted the paddle like a baseball bat just as Mark let out a chilling bark of laughter and turned his body to face the front of the boat where David and Emily lay on the deck. As the gun in his hand arched towards them, Lisa swung.

The maniacal smile of triumph was on his face when the edge of the paddle blade struck him in the bridge of his nose. With the same crazy expression on his face, he staggered back and dropped in a heap on the deck.

No one moved for what seemed to Emily an hour. Lisa stood above Mark's body with the paddle gripped tightly in her white-knuckled hands. Her chest was heaving and she seemed to be waiting for him to get up. It was her soft whimper that broke the spell and Emily shoved David off of her and struggled to her feet. She rushed to Lisa and put out her hand to touch her but stopped short of the girl's arm. The whimpering had changed to a keening wail and the sound sliced through Emily's heart. She stepped past her and stood between Lisa and Mark's body to block the girl's view. When Lisa raised her head and met Emily's, the look was one of such devastation it took her breath away. Emily reached out and gently pulled Lisa's hands away from the handle of the paddle and handed it off to David, who had stepped up beside her. Lisa looked at her empty hands and seemed to deflate into herself. She wrapped her arms around her body and started to rock back and forth. Emily stepped up to her and pulled her into an embrace and felt tears pouring down her own face.

She turned Lisa away from Mark as Mason and David crouched down to check on him. It didn't take long for David to look up at her and shake his head. Emily looked away. Mark and Tim were both dead and they would have to find a way through this nightmare.

David and Mason moved to the back of the boat and scanned the sea for any sign of Tim's body but neither boy could see him. They looked back at the girls and both felt lost at what they should do next. Mason's eyes kept drifting back to Mark's body and he finally had to speak.

"I can't believe this. He shot Tim. He killed him! Where did he even get a gun from?"

David explained about the convenience store clerk and what Emily and he had suspected. Mason had a fierce frown on his face when he stepped over Mark and looked at Lisa. She had her head buried against Emily's neck but her crying had quieted.

"Lisa, it's okay. You did the right thing. You were just trying to stop him," he said quietly with compassion.

The last thing any of them expected from Lisa was her response to his soft words. Her head came up and she pushed Emily away from her. The sorrow-filled eyes had been replaced with ones filled with rage.

"It's not okay! I want him to die! Is he dead? Did I kill him?" She half-screamed, half-sobbed. "Don't tell me it's okay! It isn't; nothing is ever going to be okay again! You used me like I was nothing so he thought he could too, except he held a gun to my head while he did it. I will never let anyone take that from me again. Never!"

Mason stumbled back. His face drained of all colour when the realization of what Lisa said sunk in. He flashed back to what Mark had said the night before about Lisa being back on the market. He remembered his flip words of "good luck". Mark had raped Lisa and it was all his fault. Mason's stomach heaved and he rushed to the rail to empty his churning guts into the sea.

Lisa walked away to the front of the boat and settled down on the deck. Emily's head ached from her words and what had just happened. David put his arms around her and pulled her into a hug. She laid her head against his chest and just breathed. She said the only thing in her mind at that moment.

"I just want to go home."

It took a while before anyone moved from their spots. They all were trying to process what had happened and more importantly, what to do next. It was Emily that finally moved first. Standing in David's embrace had helped but her eyes kept going to Mark's body and she finally couldn't take it anymore. She stepped back from David and asked,

"Should we put him overboard?"

David looked from Emily to Mason and then down at the body. He scrubbed at his face and then nodded.

"Okay, I'll help you," Emily started to offer but was interrupted by Mason.

"No. I'll do it. This is my fault. I'll deal with him," he said firmly.

Emily was going to argue that but David shook his head at her. Mason stepped over to the body and leaned down to hook his arms under Mark's armpits. He got him a foot off the deck but couldn't do more than drag him towards the rail. David stepped in and grabbed Mark's trailing feet and together they lifted him up and got him over the rail and dropped him over the side. All three of them stood there for a few minutes, each trying to come to terms in their own minds with what they had just seen. Emily sighed and turned away from the empty sea. She looked towards the front of the boat and realized that Lisa was gone. The girl must have gone below while they were dealing with Mark's body. Looking down at the deck, it took a few more seconds for Emily to understand that it wasn't only Lisa that was gone. The gun was gone too.

Chapter 14

Mason moved back to the wheel, unlocked it and checked their heading. He was trying hard to suppress the panic he was feeling about being the only one on board with any knowledge of sailing. Tim had done all the hard work. He had shown and explained everything to Mason but that didn't make him confident to do it all himself. What Mason really wanted to do was heave to and just sit for a few hours to think things through, but stopping the boat was a lot of work in itself and he knew he would have to do it before dark anyway. They were underway with a good wind and except for trimming the sails he knew that they could continue this way for a while. It was all the other things that were filling his mind. Tacking was a lot of work and the others had always been sent down to the cabin when Tim was doing this so they would be out of the way and not get conked in the head by the boom. Mason knew he could do it but was scared out of his mind at the prospect.

David came to stand by him and looked back at the way they had come. He put his hands on the rail and stared over the side down at the water.

"Do you think we should go back and try to find Tim?"

Mason shook his head sadly. "I think he was dead before he even went over. The shot took him right in the chest. He wouldn't have made it."

David nodded. "Yeah, that's what I thought but it just feels so wrong to not try. He was a really good guy. He took on a bunch of strangers and tried to help get us home. He didn't deserve to die like that especially so close to land." David lowered his head in grief but it was quickly replaced by anger. "What the hell was wrong with Mark? Why did he do that?" he asked fiercely.

Mason met his angry look with sorrow. "I don't know. I don't think I ever knew him. He was just a guy on the team. We never really talked about much except the game or going to parties. It wasn't until yesterday that I realized how little I knew him." Mason looked away but not before David saw the shame fill his eyes.

David studied Mason, trying to understand him. The cocky, selfish quarterback he had always been was no more. Everything that had made up the guy's life was gone. No more football, no girlfriend, no Lisa and now his "best friend" had turned into a monster and was dead. David felt sympathy for Mason but also knew that some of those losses were his own fault.

"Had Mark said anything to you about Tim?" David asked.

Mason couldn't meet David's eyes as he told him their plans. "We had talked about taking the boat. After, I mean. Once we hit land and Tim left, we were going to come back and take it and sail it up the coast to get closer to home. You have to believe me! We never planned to do this! I didn't know he was a psychopath. I knew he was a bully but he had never hurt anyone before. It was always just funny. Ever since we got on the boat he had taken it to the extreme. I mean, we talked about taking the boat after Tim was gone so he goes and kills him? He asked me if Lisa was back on the market last night and I was being sarcastic when I said, "good luck with that" so he rapes her. I didn't know any of this would happen! I didn't know!" he ended on a wail.

David closed his eyes in exhaustion. There was a load of grief and guilt on Mason's shoulders. Some of it was deserved, but not the horrific acts that Mark had committed. There was nothing he could say right now to help him. It was something they would all need to talk about down the road but right now they had to make plans for how to proceed. David awkwardly reached out and patted the guy on the arm.

"We need to figure out what we are going to do. I know Tim was teaching you a lot about sailing but do you think you can handle it?" At Mason's sharp nod, he continued, "We all need to sit down and talk about what we are going to do. I know this will sound harsh but with Tim gone, we don't need to sail to Washington do we?

Can we change course and head to British Colombia? Is that something you know how to do?" At another brisk nod from Mason, David sighed and went on. "Okay, I'm here to help Mason. Just tell me what to do. Tim said we would be stopping at night from now on so why don't we plan to all eat supper together and we can go over everything." When Mason didn't respond, David blurted out, "It's not your fault! You couldn't have known what Mark was going to do. Let it go for now, Mason. We need to focus on right now and getting to land."

When Mason finally met David's eyes there were tears shimmering in them. He nodded again and let out a choked, "Thank you."

David softened and threw an arm around his shoulders. "We will get home, Mason, together." They stood like that for a few minutes before David wondered where Emily had gone.

** ** ** ** ** ** ** ** ** **

Emily went down the steps to the cabin and paused at the bottom. She tried to calm her pounding heart. Lisa had been totally wrecked when she was up on deck so for her to have taken the gun was probably not a good thing. Emily was scared out of her mind with the thoughts of being on this boat with no real captain and adding an unstable girl with a gun to the mix didn't make it any better. Being as settled as she was going to get, she turned to the door of the room that she and Lisa had been sharing.

The door was slightly ajar and she gently pushed it open. The bed was empty and unmade with the sheets and blankets shoved into a pile on the foot of it. Emily stepped into the room and turned her head away from the bed. Lisa was sitting in the small armchair facing the bed. The girl was staring at the bed with a look of blank indifference on her face. The gun rested loosely in her hands in her lap. For some reason the look on her face worried Emily more than tears would have. Taking a deep breath, she stepped into the room and sat on the bed directly in front of Lisa.

Emily struggled to find the words to reach Lisa. The expression on her face told Emily that the girl was close to letting go of all hope. She sorted through the words in her head, words of comfort, of consoling and rejected them all. She felt frustrated and angry at everything that had happened today and decided to just go with harsh bluntness.

"So, are you going to kill yourself or not?" Emily asked in a flat voice.

The shock of the cruel words had Lisa's head whipping up and her eyes widened in surprise.

Before she could say anything, Emily continued.

"I mean, what's one more death today? Tim's gone, Mark, that bastard is dead and by the way, thanks for that. You probably saved my life and David's life. I'm sure we were next on his to do list. So are you going to add yourself to the list? Because I'm really ready for this day to end."

Lisa sat opened mouth with shock at Emily's harsh words. She finally managed to get herself together and speak.

"Why shouldn't I? I'm useless," she breathed out in a choked whisper.

Emily nodded thoughtfully. "Is that what you want to be? Because killing yourself would be just about the most useless thing you could do right now. Look Lisa, what Mark did to you was horrific. No one should have to go through that, but instead of cowering in the corner like a useless person, you stepped up and took the power back from him. Not only that but you stepped between him and your friends and protected them. That's not something that a useless person would do. You have a choice now. You can stand with me, with us, and fight for our lives and fight our way home or you can do the easy thing and check out. You are the only person who can make that decision but I would really like it if you stood with me."

Emily held her breath in fear at Lisa's reaction to her words. Was she too harsh? Would she make the right choice?

Lisa had dropped her head again and stared at the gun that she turned over and over in her hands. Emily could see the tears dripping off the girl's face and had to struggle not to reach out in comfort. This was something Lisa had to do herself. Emily slowly let the air out of her lungs when Lisa finally held out her hands towards her with the gun lightly resting in them. She reached out with both hands and used one to take the gun and put it behind her on the bed. With the other she pulled Lisa to her and the girl collapsed against her sobbing. It wasn't long before Emily's tears joined hers. The two girls held onto each other and sobbed out their sorrow for all they had lost, all that had been taken from them and the uncertainty of where they were going.

Chapter 15

The girls stayed down in the cabin for the rest of the day. Emily went up briefly to take the boys some food and bring down the last of the dried clothes. Mason had been giving instructions to David on how to trim the sails and Emily was reassured by his confident tone. Emily stripped the bed of the sheets in Lisa and her room and made it up with the clean bedding she found in the small storage cupboard in the room. Taking the gun off the bed, Emily stuffed it deep in a drawer under some clothes. She didn't want Lisa to have to deal with the task. After that, they worked side by side tidying up the cabin and re-sorting the supplies that they still had. They knew they were getting closer to shore and they had to decide what to take with them once they left the boat. As they worked they talked to each other about their lives. Emily was surprised by Lisa's revelations of her home life. She had no idea that Lisa's mother was such a cold perfectionist. It gave her a better understanding of why Lisa acted the way she did. She couldn't help but feel lucky with her kind, supportive parents. They had always supported and encouraged her in anything she set her mind to. Emily couldn't help but wonder how Lisa's mother was surviving in this new world without electricity. When she asked Lisa, the girl laughed without humour.

"I don't even know if my dad was home. He was away in the city more than he was ever at the house. Knowing my mother, she would have flirted or charmed some man into doing the heavy lifting. If there's one thing you can count on with her, it's that she can manipulate some guy into taking care of her. I'm pretty sure that's how she got my father. I don't think there are any real feelings between them. At least I've never seen any on display." She shook her head. "Honestly? I'm not all that excited to be in the same house as her in this new reality."

They continued to share details about each other's life and slowly the two girls saw each other with a new respect. Emily showed Lisa how to make a simple soup from the limited amount of ingredients they had, then whipped up a small batch of biscuits to put in the small oven under the stove. It didn't surprise Emily that Lisa had no knowledge of cooking but she was happy at the interest that the girl showed at learning.

After closing the oven door, Emily looked up and smiled at her new friend. Lisa still looked haggard but she was starting to get some colour back into her cheeks. The dark circles around her eyes would hopefully go away with some rest. She had seen tears come into her eyes throughout the afternoon but they never fell. It was going to take time to heal the wounded shadows in her eyes. Emily knew she had to broach a difficult subject before the boys came down to eat. They had to talk about Mason. After everything that had happened today they all had to work together if they were going to make it home.

"Lisa, I know you blame Mason for part of what happened. I think you guys are going to have to talk about things. There are only four of us left and once we get off this boat we have to work together. I'm not asking you to forgive him but you do need to talk to him."

Lisa sighed sadly and looked away. "What I said before, on deck, I didn't really mean. I know it wasn't his fault what Mark did. It wasn't even all his fault what happened between us either. I was the one that kept going to him. I guess I just needed someone to focus all my anger on. I'll talk to him. I don't know if we can ever be friends but we'll work together. None of that really even matters anymore. I'm finally realizing that all the petty high school drama is over. This is real life now and I'm going to try my hardest to survive it." She turned to Emily and met her compassionate eyes. "I just want to thank you for what you did earlier. I think I would have done something really stupid if you hadn't said what you did. I just…I owe you. You saved my life right back," she ended on a whisper.

Reaching out, Emily squeezed Lisa's hand and said, "I think we might have more lifesaving in the future so I'm glad you decided to stay."

It wasn't too long after that conversation that the wonderful smell of baking biscuits filled the cabin. As if it was a signal, the girls felt the motion of the boat change and guessed that they were going to stop for the night. They had been sailing almost constantly since they left land and they really felt the difference in the boat's rocking in the waves. Emily steadied herself against the counter as David came bounding down the stairs from above. His serious face was topped by wind-blown hair. He offered Emily a quick smile and nodded at Lisa.

"Mason is doing something called heaving to which I'm guessing is sort of parking the boat for the night. He will be down in a minute. Wow, something smells amazing!"

Emily smiled, "Good timing. Lisa and I made supper and the biscuits should be just about done. Man, I never knew how much I could miss butter but we can use jam or peanut butter on them."

David looked at Lisa in surprise. "Hey, that's great. Thanks, you guys. I will happily take fresh bread any way I can get it!"

Lisa nodded shyly and went to help Emily ladle out bowls of soup. There were rubber place mats on the table that helped to keep the dishes from sliding on the table. They really helped as the boat moved up and down with each wave.

Mason came down the stairs and moved to the table just as Lisa placed the plate of hot biscuits on it. He looked up at her in surprise before quickly looking away. Everyone could feel the tension in the room. Until Lisa and Mason talked things out everyone would be uncomfortable. It was David that broke the silence after a few minutes of eating.

"So we need to talk about where we are going from here. It's awful what happened to Tim and I would do anything to change it but we can't. I really wish there was some way we could let his family know what happened to him. He deserves so much more than what happened to him but there's nothing we can do and with him gone we have no reason to go to Washington anymore. If we change our course we can head northeast and try to sail up to British Columbia. If we can land somewhere south of Vancouver, it will save us weeks of travelling by foot. What do you guys think?"

Mason was the first to reply. "I will look over the charts that Tim has onboard but I'm a little nervous about sailing between Vancouver Island and Seattle. There's lots of room at first but then there are a lot of little islands all through there. I really don't think I'm confident enough to sail through that. It would be a disaster if we wrecked the boat on one of them and were stuck with no way to get off."

Everyone was surprised when Lisa spoke up. There was so much tension between the two that no one expected her to talk to him. She didn't look at him as she spoke.

"We have all that gas. Why don't we switch to the motor when we get close to them and not worry about using the sails? That way you would have more control of the boat."

There was silence around the table as Emily and David looked at Mason and waited for his reply. He sent a tentative smile at Lisa before quickly looking away from her intense stare.

"You're totally right. It would give us more control. I would have to do the math on how far we could go on what we have but I think we should be fine. We did take a lot of extra from the other boats back in the marina. Thanks, Lisa," he ended softly.

David was nodding and was about to speak when Lisa cleared her throat. All eyes went to her.

She looked at everyone around the table and then dropped her eyes to her lap. "I just wanted to say a few things. I know I haven't been the most useful person on the trip so far and I haven't really contributed but I'm going to change. I..." Her speech stalled as she tried to find the words. Before she was ready, Mason jumped in.

"Lisa, I'm sorry. I'm so sorry for what I did to you. It's my fault that Mark hurt you. If I could go back and change things, I would do it in a heartbeat. You didn't deserve what happened and I'm going to try my hardest to protect you and take care of you and get you home safe! I hope one day you can forgive me."

David and Emily's heads swiveled towards Lisa to see how she would respond to his heartfelt admission. Lisa had tears trickling down her face and she brushed them away before raising her head and looking directly at Mason. She took a deep breath.

"It wasn't your fault. We haven't been very nice people and we have both done really stupid things. Mark did what he did because he was evil. He wanted to be in control of us and he was jealous of you. From some of the things he told me, I know he would have made a move no matter what happened. He was a really damaged guy and no matter what he did, I will have to live with killing him. It wasn't your fault, Mason."

Mason's eyes had tears in them. They both sat silently. David looked at Emily and she shrugged. This was something that Mason and Lisa would have to work together to get through. After a few moments of silence, David started talking.

"I don't think anyone knew that Mark would go psycho. Lisa, I really don't think you should feel guilty for killing him. After what he did to you and Tim, he would have come after me. So you probably saved my life. I'm not saying that killing someone is okay but I really believe that you did the right thing. If I had had the chance, I would have thrown him overboard after what he did. You did the right thing. Mason, Mark made his own choices. No matter what happened before, he made the choice to hurt people so stop blaming yourself. What happened between you and Lisa is between you two but you guys need to talk about it and get past it. I know I've said it before but I'm going to say it again. After we get off this boat, we need to work together. We have to trust each other and watch out for each other. We're just teenagers. We aren't trained commandos or fighters and we might have to fight so we need to count on each other. If we are fighting with each other then we won't make it. So, from now on we are a team and we work together and help each other or we might as well go our separate ways once we hit land. Do you guys agree?"

Everyone nodded their heads so after a minute David leaned over the map and they got to work.

It wasn't very late before everyone started to yawn and feel the effects of the emotional day. After cleaning up the supper dishes, they made a plan to start packing up supplies in the morning and they all went to bed. Emily wasn't sure if Lisa would want to sleep in the room where Mark had hurt her but she followed Emily into the room. Once they had settled into bed, they both stared at the ceiling, each girl lost in thoughts of the day they had just lived through. The sound of Lisa crying brought Emily back to the present and she reached across the bed and took hold of her hand. Lisa squeezed back and tried to get control of her tears.

"Emily, I'm scared," she whispered.

Emily closed her eyes, "Me too."

"Will you help me? I…I don't know anything. I don't even know how to cook food. I don't want to be taken care of. I want to learn to take care of myself. I never want to be dependent on anyone to survive."

Emily nodded her head in the dark. "I'll help you, Lisa. I'll teach you as much as I can but there's something you need to understand. In this new world, we are all going to be dependent on each other. I don't think anyone can survive on their own. What's important is picking the right people to depend on and giving back as much as they give. Being taken care of isn't a weakness when you take care of each other. It has a name. It's called family and that's what we are now. The four of us, we are a family."

The two girls laid there holding hands thinking about that term and it comforted them as they fell asleep.

Chapter 16

They got a late start the next morning. After a quick breakfast of leftover biscuits with jam and peanut butter, they all sorted through their belongings and supplies to determine what they would take with them when they left the boat. With only four people to carry supplies, they wouldn't be able to take as much as they would like. Emily knew they would take the backpacks that they had already packed and attached to the life boat but she was wracking her brain to find a way to take more. What they really needed was a way to transport the extra supplies. She discussed the idea with David and they decided to try and find a wagon, stroller or shopping cart once they landed before they all left the boat for good. Mason spent some time studying the maps and charts that were onboard to plot out their new course. His best guess was that it would take them an extra two days to go further north and land them on the B.C. coast. Once he was finished with the charts, he and David went up on deck to get underway. There wasn't much more that they could do until they actually came ashore so the girls went up on deck as well once Mason had gotten them up to speed.

The sun was shining bright and clear but there was a build up of clouds in the distance. There wasn't much conversation as they sailed closer to land. The events of the previous day weighed heavily on them all. It would be a long time before Emily got the sound of the gunshot and the image of Tim flipping over the rail and into the ocean out of her head. Tim's death filled her with so much sadness and guilt. He had been such a nice man and she felt partly responsible for his death. She remembered sitting in the golf cart with David and deciding to split from the others after Mason had left her in the street. If she had followed through with that, Tim wouldn't have taken them on his boat and he would still be alive.

Sighing deeply, she looked at the others spread out on the deck. Lisa was staring out to sea and Emily could only imagine what must be going through her head. She had suffered major emotional trauma. Having been raped and then having to kill would damage anyone. Emily had seen a new side of Lisa before those events had happened and she admired the core of strength that the girl had shown by not taking the easy way out or reverting back to the shallow, useless person she had been previously. It took a lot of guts and strength to make it through what she had and become a better person. Emily knew in her heart that she and Lisa would grow closer and be there for each other.

Looking back at Mason, she saw that he was frowning in concentration at the wheel. He had said all the right words about being a different person but Emily knew it would be hard to trust him fully until he proved that they could count on him.

David stood tall at the mast, scanning the sea ahead of them. He was her biggest comfort in the whole mess of this trip. He had not had the easiest life, but he was a strong and loyal friend. She marveled that he wasn't full of anger and bitterness. After his father had left for the final time, his mom had struggled with depression herself. He had stepped up and looked after himself and his little sister, Emma. Even after his mom found her feet and moved on from the loss, he had taken so many responsibilities on himself. They had scaled down their farm quite a bit, but there was still so much work that he took care of himself after his mom had to get a job in town. Emily knew that David harboured a lot of anger and disappointment towards his dad but he never let it affect his attitude towards others or life in general. She was just so thankful that he had come with her when she had split from the rest of their friends.

Emily looked out at the ocean and wished for land. She knew how much harder it would have been to walk the huge distance that they had traveled by boat but she was sick of the water and wanted to be on land. She had to laugh at the irony of that. Her biggest passion was swimming through the water and here she wanted to get away from it. Shaking her head at the way life could change, she stood up and headed towards the cabin steps. Making food and cleaning up at least helped to pass the time. She was almost to the stairs when David called out for the binoculars. Grabbing them quickly she returned to David and handed them to him.

After looking through them for a few minutes he handed them back to her. "Take a look. There's a boat ahead of us. It looks like a cabin cruiser and I can see at least two people on board. It's still too far away to see clearly who they are. Keep an eye on it. I'm going to talk to Mason and we should decide what we want to do."

"What do you mean what we should do? These are the first people we have seen alive since we set sail. Aren't we going to stop and talk to them? They might be stuck out here. We need to help them!" Emily exclaimed.

"I know, Em, but they might not be friendly. We have to be careful. If we stop and they try and take the boat from us, we could be in a huge amount of trouble. We need to be smart about this so keep watching and let us know what you see, okay?"

Nodding her head in understanding, Emily brought the glasses up to her eyes and tried to focus on the boat that was ahead of them. She could see it but the details weren't clear. There was definitely movement on its deck but they weren't close enough to see who it was. She looked away when she heard Mason, Lisa and David arguing.

"I'm just saying that we are so close to land that it would be stupid to take such a chance!" Mason argued.

"That is so selfish! What if those people have been stranded out here the whole time? Don't you remember the life boats with all those dead people? We have to help them. It's the right thing to do!" Lisa said forcefully.

"Whoa, cool it down guys! You are both right. We need to be careful and find out who is on that boat and help them if they are in trouble. So, we go in slow and keep our distance until we know the situation. Then, if it looks safe, we will do what we can to help them," David intervened.

"No way, man, this is a bad idea! We only have so much food and water for ourselves. We can't just be giving it away," Mason protested.

Before David and Lisa could start in, Emily pushed past them and got into Mason's face.

"How dare you? A good man took us in and helped us when he could have just left us to die in that city. We repaid him by killing him. Mark might have pulled the trigger but we were the ones that brought him onto the boat. We owe Tim and we need to repay his kindness. We will help these people if it looks safe because it's the right thing to do and because that's what Tim did for us. If you can't understand that then you really are an asshole and I don't want anything to do with you!" Emily's chest was heaving with anger and Mason took a step back with shock from her words.

"Emily...I...I'm sorry. I know it's the right thing to do, it's just...I'm scared!" he said softly with shame.

Emily's face relaxed slightly. "Yeah, well, so am I. I'm scared every minute of every day but that doesn't change the fact that helping those people is the right thing to do." She heaved out a breath. "Slow us down and switch to the engine or whatever it is that you have to do but get it done. We are getting closer and we need to be able to manoeuvre closer or away depending on what we find," she ordered and walked away.

Lisa followed her down into the cabin and they gathered water bottles and power bars together. They felt the speed of the boat drop as Mason and David adjusted the sails. As Emily added the first aid kit to the bag they were going to take on deck, she felt the vibrations of the engine as Mason fired it up. The girls were about to go back on deck when she heard David call out. As they rushed up the stairs to see what was going on, Emily came to a dead stop and spun around, almost knocking Lisa back down. She thrust the bag of supplies at her.

"Here, take this up. I forgot something. Be right up!" she said as she pushed past her and ran back down into the cabin. Making her way quickly in to the main bedroom she ran to the dresser and reached out to yank one of the drawers open. She paused for a minute as her head whirled with possible scenarios of what they might find on the other boat. She shook her head abruptly at her indecision and pulled the drawer out. Reaching under the folded clothing, she grasped the cold metal of the gun and pulled it out. It was a simple revolver and she could see that there were five bullets in the chambers. She kicked herself for not searching through Mark's things to see if he had any more bullets hidden. Emily studied the gun for a few minutes. She had fired many rifles and shot guns in her young life on a farm but she had never fired a handgun. She closed her eyes briefly and prayed that today wouldn't be the day that she would. She quickly stuffed it in to her pocket and pulled her shirt out so it would hang down and cover the bulge and then flew back out into the cabin and up the stairs.

Mason was at the wheel and he locked eyes with her the minute she stepped on deck.

"Emily, I sorry, you were right." he said seriously.

"I know, Mason, but we need to be stronger and make better decisions," she said distractedly, trying to adjust her shirt to cover her front pocket.

"I know but that's not what I meant. That boat has little kids on it. We do have to help them," he explained.

"What? Oh no! I hope they are okay." Emily whirled around to get a look at the boat they were slowly approaching with concern on her face. She couldn't imagine how scary being stranded at sea would be for little kids. She almost went back into the cabin to return the gun to the drawer but decided she could do that after. She moved towards the bow of the boat where Lisa and David were standing. Lisa was waving at the two kids who were watching them come closer with scared little faces. She scanned the rest of the boat looking for their parents but the deck was empty.

Emily turned to David who had a frown on his face and asked, "Their parents?"

He shook his head. "I haven't seen any adults so far, just the two kids but we don't know if anyone is in the cabin."

"Why wouldn't they come up with the kids?"

"I don't know. Maybe they're hurt or sick. We'll have to wait and see. But Emily, this feels wrong."

Emily frowned and turned back to look at the children. They were close enough to see that it was a little girl who looked about eight or nine and a smaller boy who might have been six. They both looked scared which confused Emily even more. If the kids were stuck out here alone then why would they be scared of other people? Why wouldn't they be happy or excited or even relieved that there were people here that could help them? She was about to say as much to David when she felt the engine stop and Mason came forward with the long handled paddle. As they drifted closer he leaned out and used the paddle to hook onto the other boat so they were closer and quickly dropped it and tied the two boats together.

Lisa was trying to talk soothingly to the kids but they just stepped back away from the rail and said nothing.

"It's okay, we can help you. Do you need help? We have food and water. Are your parents on board? Is anyone hurt? We can help you." Lisa tried to get a response but the kids just backed away further. She turned to look at the others. "They are terrified but I don't know why. They're dirty but they don't seen hurt. Maybe you should try talking to them, Emily."

Emily nodded and reached down to brace herself on the rail so she could swing across to the other boat when David grabbed her arm. She looked up at him in confusion but he wasn't looking at her. He was staring hard at something on the other boat. She turned her head and found herself looking down the barrel of a shotgun.

Chapter 17

"Don't even move!" said a harsh voice from behind the gun.

Emily straightened up despite the order and saw a scruffy man who hadn't showered in days. His eyes were fierce and they held depths of desperation.

She looked at the kids now standing behind him and they still looked scared. The little boy was quietly crying into the girl's side. The girl met Emily's look and she could see a hint of steel in her eyes. Looking back at the man, she tried to reason with him.

"Mister, do you guys need any help? We saw the kids on deck and came to offer food and water if you need it. If you are stranded we could take you to shore. You don't need to point that gun at us."

The gun never wavered as he let out a bitter laugh. "Oh yeah, that's what the last people who stopped to "help" said before they took all of our supplies and my wife. So yeah, I'll accept your help. I'll accept that boat you're on and everything in it as well."

Emily glanced at the others and saw Lisa frozen in shock. Mason was scowling and David was shaking his head. He tried talking to the man.

"Sir, you don't have to do that. We will share everything we have and help you and your kids get to land. We stopped to help you guys!"

The man nodded his head determinedly. "A week ago I would have taken you up on that but now it's too late. I'm all my kids have left and I will do anything to keep them safe. So I want all of you to back up and stand together near the mast. Don't try anything or I'll shoot!" he gestured with the gun barrel further back on the boat.

David put his hand on Emily's shoulder from behind and pulled her gently back away from the edge of the boat. Once they had all moved back, David stepped in front of her so he was between her and the gun.

The man kept his gun on them as he quickly manoeuvred over the rail and on to the Lawless. Once he was braced on their deck, he scanned it from side to side. Lisa was clutching the bag to her chest and he nodded at her.

"What's in the bag?"

Lisa looked down at it with a blank look until she realized he was talking to her and then her expression turned into an angry scowl.

"This is the food and water we gathered to help your family. Guess you want that too!" she spat at him.

The man almost looked ashamed for a second before his face hardened again.

"No, you hold on to that for now." He looked the others over and addressed David. "Who else is on board?"

David shook his head. "There isn't anyone else. We all came up to help you guys."

The man frowned again and Emily was getting the feeling that he wasn't as hard as he was pretending to be. He glanced back at his kids and waved the girl forward.

"Sarah, come over here and go around the other side of the cabin. Take a quick look down there and make sure no one else is onboard with us. Ben, stay there for a minute until Sarah comes back," he told the crying boy when he tried to follow his sister over the rail.

Sarah scampered over the rail easily and ran around the opposite side of the boat to reach the stairs. No one said anything while she was out of sight. When she popped back up on deck, she gave her Dad a nod and ran back around to stand by him. He took a deep breath and told them what to do.

"You guys are going to cross over onto my boat and stay there. You can take that bag of food and water with you. I'm sure someone will come along and find you. I've set up rain water traps so you should be okay for water. I would ration the food though. There's none on board. There are two fishing rods so you can try and fish." He turned to his kids and instructed them. "Sarah, Ben, get down to our cabin and get some of your clothes and anything else you want. Sarah, grab some of my stuff too. Be fast."

~ 129 ~

The girl still hadn't spoken and she just nodded and jumped back onto her boat and dragged her brother down below.

Emily looked at the man and decided to try and reason with him again. She slid around David and gave the man her most sincere expression.

"Sir, I'm sorry about what happened to your family but we aren't a threat to you. We're just a bunch of teenagers trying to get home. We were in Disneyland when everything stopped and we found a boat to try and get home. We live in Alberta, Canada and if you leave us out here we will never see our parents again. Please don't do this. We are only a day or two from land. Just tie us up and take us with you. We won't cause you any problems. I promise!" she begged with tears in her eyes.

The man closed his eyes in sadness but slowly shook his head. In a soft voice he told her, "I'm sorry. I just can't take that chance. I'm not a bad man and I don't want to hurt you kids but I have to make sure my kids are safe. I'm really sorry. I wish there was a different way." His eyes pleaded with Emily to understand.

David spoke from behind her. "Sir, we can see that you are trying to protect your family and that's the right thing to do but if you leave us on that boat we will probably die. That would make you a murderer. There is a different way that would give us a chance. Let us take our life boat. We could try rowing it to land. It would take us a long time but at least we would be moving. Your boat is dead in the water, we wouldn't get anywhere in it. Let us take the life boat and you can keep both boats. Please, sir. Give us a chance to make it to land," he pleaded.

While the man contemplated this, Emily was trying not to freak out. What was David doing?! She couldn't get the image of the life boats filled with sunbaked dead people out of her head. She couldn't believe he had suggested that! She looked to Lisa whose mouth was hanging open in shock at David. Mason caught her eye and he gave her a brief nod. She was completely confused.

Why did the boys think that getting into the life boat was a good idea?

The man was staring at David with a thoughtful expression. "Do you really think that you can row to shore?"

David shrugged. "It's better to try than to sit and slowly go crazy waiting for someone to maybe find us."

The man nodded and gave David a grim smile. "I admire that. You're a strong boy. I hope you make it and I'm sorry."

David just nodded. "My friend and I are going to go get the life boat in the water. The girls can stay here while we do it. As soon as we get it launched, I'll come back here while my friends get onboard and then I will follow them."

The man raised his eyebrows at David's instructions. "You're awfully confident for a boy with a gun pointed at him."

David stared him down before replying. "You're not going to shoot an unarmed teenager in front of your children who's done nothing to you but offer help. Like you said, you're not a bad man…just a thief." He turned around without giving the man a chance to respond and tapped Mason to follow him. He looked at Emily and Lisa and said, "Sit tight," before going to the life boat case.

David and Mason bent over and started to undo the clasps that held the case to the boat. Without looking at Mason, David said in a low voice, "Try and block his view of the bags. I don't know if he'll try and stop us from taking them but let's not bring them to his attention."

Mason nodded and shuffled around so his body was between the attached garbage bags filled with their backpacks and the front of the boat where the man was standing. Once the case was freed from its clamps, they piled the bags on top of it and carried it to the rail. David made sure he had a tight grip on the release cord before they heaved it over the side. They watched anxiously as the case went under the water and popped back up before splitting open and inflating. Both boys let out the breaths that they had been holding. If the boat hadn't inflated they would have been stuck on the man's boat with no chance of getting to shore. David was happy to see the life boat was slightly pulled down on one side meaning that the bags of supplies were still attached.

David stood up and handed the rope to Mason. "Pull it in close and help the girls get in. I'll be back in a minute," he said before heading back to where the girls were waiting nervously. Mason nodded and started to pull the boat closer.

David joined Emily and Lisa and moved around them so that he was once again between them and the man with the gun. He gave him a cool nod before talking to the girls. Lisa had a fiercely defiant look on her face and Emily looked slightly panicked.

"It's okay, guys. Go over to Mason and he'll help you down."

Emily shot the man a nervous look over David's shoulder and then leaned in to him and whispered, "I have the gun. We have to stop him." Her eyes held a frantic look.

David froze and stared hard at her for a second. His mind flashed to all the outcomes of using the gun to defend the boat. He shook the images of screaming children and a deck covered in blood out of his head.

"No. Just go to Mason and get in the life boat," he said firmly.

Emily shook her head. "David, you saw what happened to those men in the life boats! We will die if we go out there!" she pleaded in fear.

He took a hold of her shoulders and gave them a squeeze. "Those men weren't prepared. We prepared for this, remember? We will have everything that we will need. Please, Emily, trust me," he told her quietly while staring hard into her eyes.

He turned her towards Mason and urged her on. Lisa was slowly nodding her head in understanding and she turned and followed Emily.

David watched Mason help Emily over the rail and then motion for Lisa. Once he was sure they would be okay, he turned to face the man. The children had returned to the deck of the other boat and stood watching with bags at their feet.

"A good man owned this boat. His name was Tim. He was trying to get home just like the rest of us. We were strangers but he took us with him because it was the right thing to do. One of the guys that had come with us went bad and killed him and ended up dying himself in the process. Tim lost his life because he helped us. We stopped to help you because it was, again, the right thing to do and we wanted to pay back Tim for helping us by passing it along. I want you to remember this. Today you did a bad thing for a good reason. You saved your children but you also showed them not to trust or help others. You need to make that right. So if you come across anyone who needs help in the future you should do the right thing and help them. Show your children that there is still goodness in this new messed up world."

With that said David nodded at the man, turned, and got into the life boat.

Chapter 18

Emily watched as they drifted further from the Lawless. The others were busy pulling up the bags with their backpacks in them but she was so despondent that she made no effort to help. She pulled her knees up closer to her chest and laid her head down on them. How could this have happened? Her worst nightmare had come true and all she could think about was what happened to the last life boats she had seen. She couldn't understand why David and Mason had chosen this. She also was struggling to understand how that man could do this to them after they had tried to help his family. Was this what they had to look forward to for the future? Every person for themselves and no one willing to help each other? She felt the tears slide down her face and dampen her knees. She missed her mom and dad and just wanted to go home. She felt her heart ache at the thought of never seeing them again and let out a sob.

Lisa settled down beside her and put her arm around her shoulders, trying to console her.

"It's going to be okay, Emily."

Emily lifted her tearstained face and looked at her blankly. "How is it going to be okay? We are going to die out here just like those other men we saw."

David shuffled over to her on his knees. "No, we aren't, Emily. I'm sorry I couldn't explain before we got off the Lawless but I didn't want that guy to change his mind. I know you think it was a mistake but let me explain. If we had been forced on to his boat we probably wouldn't have made it. It was dead in the water and way too big to try and row. The chances of anyone finding us on it are slim. We could have been out there for months and a bad enough storm will probably swamp and sink it. I know being on the life boat is scary, but we have a better chance. It's small and we can all take turns trying to paddle. We figured we were only a day or two from land with the Lawless, and this will take us longer, but we shouldn't be out here for more than a week. We have six

~ 134 ~

backpacks full of supplies and the emergency kit that was already on the boat. That man's boat had nothing on it for food and water. The canopy on this one will protect us from the sun and rain and we should be okay in any storms because it's light enough. We will get tossed around and it won't be fun but we shouldn't sink. Emily, we honestly have a better chance in this one." He looked to Mason for help when Emily didn't respond.

"It's true, Emily. If we were farther away from shore, I would have picked the other one and hoped for rescue but we could have sat on that boat for months slowly dying of starvation and dehydration. We have a better chance in the life boat for making it to shore. That other boat had no way to steer into the waves if there was a storm. We would have been broadsided and sunk. You also need to remember that those life boats with the dead guys were really old. They didn't have canopies on them so they were exposed to the elements," Mason explained.

Emily looked at all her friend's faces and they all seemed confident in their survival. Slowly the feeling of hopelessness eased and she took a deep breath and nodded.

"Okay, so who's paddling first?" she said with a trembling smile.

"Actually, that would be me." Lisa surprised them. At their sceptical looks, she lifted her chin. "What? I've been using the rowing machine in the gym for the past two years. It's a great workout for cheerleading. I know it's not the same as real life rowing but at least my muscles are used to that exercise. I'll bet I last longer than you boys and won't hurt as bad after," she said smugly.

Emily smiled at her friend's proud expression. "Wow, Lisa. Is that one of those skills you thought was useless?" she teased.

Lisa blushed in embarrassment. "I guess there are some things that I can help with after all."

Mason was looking at Lisa with a thoughtful expression and David was grinning. "All right then. Let's get this canopy pulled down halfway and get rowing!" David said in an upbeat tone.

Emily marvelled at how her friends were staying positive in such an uncertain situation. She firmly squared her shoulders and leaned forward to help.

** ** ** ** ** ** ** ** ** **

The sun was going down and they were all exhausted. Lisa was right about the new muscles they needed to use for rowing. It was impossible to tell if they had made any real progress, but they all felt like they had rowed miles. David checked the compass often to make sure they stayed on course. They had a simple dinner of water and beef jerky with half a power bar each for dessert. The dark clouds they had seen earlier in the day were much closer and they were all resigned to the fact that it would be raining some time tonight. Emily prayed it was only rain and not a fierce storm. She almost laughed at the irony. Two weeks on a large comfortable sail boat and they had no bad weather, but the minute they leave it they get hit with a storm. Murphy's Law was rearing its ugly head.

After they had eaten, there was some uncomfortable and embarrassing business to attend to. Going to the bathroom over the side of an inflated boat was not fun. The boys had an easier time of it but that would change once they had to do the second job. Emily and Lisa worked out a system where they held onto each other's arms while hanging over the side. It was embarrassing but with the boy's backs turned they got it done.

They all settled down for the night and David closed the canopy. It was a lot like being in a tent except for the rocking and rolling over the waves. The emotional and physical day took its toll and they all fell asleep quickly.

Emily was dreaming. She was just a little kid and she was playing on her parent's water bed. She loved the way it would roll her around when she bounced her bum on it. She was giggling in delight when the man who had forced them off the Lawless came into the room and shoved the end of the water mattress sending her flying up off the bed. Her laughter turned to screams. Emily was torn from her dream as her body crashed into Lisa's and their heads connected. Dazed from the blow, she was unable to control her body as it was sent tumbling in a different direction. She once again connected with a body but this time her head bounced off the side of the canopy. Strong hands gripped her and she was dragged up against Mason. He had anchored himself against the side of the boat and wrapped one arm around her and held on with the other.

When Emily's head cleared enough to process what was happening, she saw David holding on to Lisa, who seemed to be unconscious. The boat was being tossed all over the place and Emily closed her eyes in fear. That was a huge mistake because her stomach lurched and she couldn't control the hot wave of vomit that came rushing up her throat. She was powerless to do anything except let it out. Hot tears of misery poured down her face as her stomach heaved again and again.

Emily wasn't the only one to lose her stomach contents that long, wave-tossed night. Sleep was impossible and they were all weak with exhaustion from clinging to the sides of the boat so they wouldn't collide. Emily had no idea where David found the strength to hold onto Lisa for so many hours. The roaring wind made talking nearly impossible but he shouted out that she was breathing, just knocked out. Emily thought she might have lost her sanity if not for the small light that was clipped onto the canopy. It wasn't very bright but being able to see her friends made all the difference.

Her eyes were grainy and her head ached when the canopy slowly started to lighten and the waves calmed. She had to peel her fingers away from the handle as they were without feeling after clutching it for so long. She used her other hand to massage some feeling back into the bloodless fingers. David lay Lisa on her side and crawled over to the opening. He pulled the flap aside and tied it back. The fresh air blew in and washed away some of the vomit stench.

Emily breathed the clean air in gulps and with the sun lighting up the inside of the boat, she took stock of the night's damage. Their bags were tumbled everywhere and many of their supplies had come loose and were scattered all over the bottom of the boat. Worse was the vomit that coated almost everything. The fresh air helped to clear some of her headache and it also seemed to help revive Lisa, who let out a moan and struggled to sit up. Ignoring the mess around her, Emily scooted closer to her and helped her sit up. She winced at the bruised knot on Lisa's temple and raised her hand to gently probe the matching goose egg on her own forehead.

When Lisa's glassy eyes cleared, she looked around at the mess in the boat with confusion.

"What the heck happened?" she asked and wrinkled her nose at the foul smell.

Emily slumped down beside her. "A big storm hit us and we knocked heads when the waves tossed us. David, Mason and I all contributed to the wonderful aroma that you currently smell. How's your head?"

Lisa tentatively rubbed the lump and winced. "Um, ouch?"

"Yeah, me too. Just be grateful you weren't awake for that roller coaster ride. It went on for hours."

Emily sighed. She snagged a backpack and rummaged through it until she pulled out a bottle of aspirin. She handed Lisa two of the pills and took two of her own.

"Thank God for the canopy. If it wasn't there, we would have lost everything and probably gone over the side, too."

Lisa gave a half-hearted laugh. "Yeah, but at least it would have washed the puke away!"

Emily sent Lisa a devilish grin. "So…remember when you said you would do the laundry next time?"

Lisa started to shake her head frantically. "Oh no, no way! That's not fair. I didn't even puke. I shouldn't have to clean this up!"

Just as Lisa took a deep breath to make her case a gust of wind came into the boat and sent a strong wash of the foul air right into her face. Her eyes got huge and she lunged towards the opening but she wasn't fast enough and her vomit joined the mess that the other three had left on the bottom of the boat. After wiping her mouth on her sleeve she flopped back beside Emily.

Emily closed her eyes and shook her head. "Welcome back, Murphy!"

Chapter 19

In the end, they all helped to clean the mess. After wiping down the inside of the canopy, David tied it back almost all the way. They used ocean water to wash everything as their drinking water was too precious to waste, mopping the bottom of the boat as best they could with one of the few towels they had packed and taking turns leaning over the side to wash out clothes. When Emily felt the sticky mess in her hair, she gave up trying to clean over the side and just jumped over into the water.

The shock of the cold water cleared the last of the pain from her head and after dunking repeatedly she felt her hair was puke-free. Once she got used to the temperature, she enjoyed treading water. It had been weeks since she was in a pool and she hadn't realized how much she had missed it. Even so, she knew she couldn't stay in the water very long or she would risk hypothermia. Scrubbing her clothes as best she could she stripped off under water and handed them up to Lisa who wrung them out and spread them out to dry in the sun. When she was down to her bra and underwear, she asked the boys to turn around so she could get back in. Lisa was ready with the other towel they had and she had gotten Emily's spare clothing out also.

Emily heaved up onto the side of the boat and rolled over the edge. When Lisa wrapped the towel around her she saw that Emily's teeth were chattering and her lips had a slight blue hue to them.

"Get that wet stuff off and pull on some dry clothes. I'll hold the blanket up for you. You're freezing!" Lisa said with concern.

Emily nodded and quickly wrung out her hair over the side before rubbing her chilled skin with the towel and diving into her clean clothes. She hadn't thought she would get cold after such a quick dip. She and Alex and their other friends had plenty of experience swimming in cold Alberta lakes but she had never done it before the end of May. After dressing, she wrapped the towel around her wet hair and tried to rub out as much water as possible. Lisa draped the blanket she had been holding up around her shoulders and settled down beside her.

"I was going to jump in after you were done but after seeing your blue lips, I think I'll pass." Lisa said.

Emily nodded. "Yeah, I don't think I'll be doing that again! Holy cow! That was brutal cold but at least the puke is gone. Now I just have a layer of salt on me."

She dived into her backpack again and came out with some toilet paper. She moistened it with a little bottled water and ran it over her face and hands. Taking out the baggie of sunscreen, she was thankful it hadn't broken open during the storm and coated everything in the bag. She worked the cream into her face and hands before handing it to Lisa so she could do the same.

The boys had finished washing out their stuff on the other side and Lisa carefully passed the floppy bag of cream over to David so he and Mason could coat their unprotected skin. Once they had repacked the supplies that had needed to be cleaned off and draped their clothes out to dry they settled down for food and water. There was no chance of making anything close to a real meal but the water and granola bars were enough to sooth their aching bellies. The almost continuous dry heaving they had done in the storm had taken its toll.

There was no way of knowing where they were after the storm had tossed them around, but the sun was still rising and they could use that and the compass for direction. Emily was adamant that they all coat themselves with sunscreen and wear the hats she had packed. The ocean breeze kept them cool but the sun baked down on them.

Lisa once again started off paddling, impressing Emily and the others. With all the aches and pains from being tossed around the night before Emily felt the soreness in her arms the most and didn't mind a little more rest.

Mason and David tried use the canopy as a type of sail but didn't have much luck. They could tell that they were moving east but there was no way to tell how fast they were going or the exact direction. It was frustrating not having more control but Mason was quick to point out that it was better than sitting dead in the water. Emily tried to see it that way but she kept getting images in her head of them floating all the way back to California. She tried to stay calm and focused but after twenty-four hours at the mercy of the sea she was anxious and restless, constantly scanning in all directions for dark clouds. She tried to distract herself by thinking about what was happening at home but that just filled her with sadness and longing. The same feelings hit her when she tried to guess where Alex and the others would be by now. After being away from land for so long, it was easy to dream about what was happening there. She imagined that there would be refugee camps and military people helping to put things in order. Her fondest wish was that they would get to shore and find out that only California had been affected. Finally shaking her head, she focused on the people with her.

Lisa had really surprised her. She had changed from a selfish, spoiled diva to a friend and helper. If anything, she was doing better than Emily was. David's calmness never cracked. He just kept on going and took every hit in stride.

She looked at him now and smiled at his sun-kissed hair. The muscles on his arms flexed as he rowed and when he turned his head and met her eyes, the concentrating seriousness on his face changed to a smile. When she smiled back, she felt a flutter in her belly and she looked away in confusion. David had always been one of her best friends but as the days passed she found herself looking at him differently. Had she been so blinded by Mason that she had overlooked what was right in front of her? When she felt a feeling of regret, she shoved it aside. This wasn't the time or place to even think about these things. Even so, when she glanced back at him she couldn't help but wonder if she was that clueless. Turning away again, her gaze fell on Mason. She was still on the fence about him. She had seen all his sides and hoped they could trust him but she just wasn't sure. He had strongly objected to stopping to help the people they had lost the Lawless to and in hindsight he had been right but he hadn't said one word about it.

"Mason, I'm sorry we didn't listen to you. You were right." she said abruptly.

He looked at her in confusion. "About what?" he asked.

"You didn't want us to stop and help those people and you were right. We lost our boat because of it so I'm sorry."

Mason started to shake his head. "No, no way. I was wrong, Emily. I was being selfish and scared. Even though we lost the boat, it was still the right thing to do. I've made a lot of bad choices in the past but I don't want to be that person anymore. We tried to help and do the right thing. There was no way we could have known it would turn out that way."

Emily's respect for Mason went up a notch at his admission and David and Lisa nodded as well. If they made it to shore there would be other situations that they would face when it came to helping others. Emily knew that they would be more cautious in the future but they would still try and help others if they could. Despite their current situation, she knew that they had been lucky so far. They'd had very little physical hardship and they had been eating well. She knew that millions of people couldn't say the same.

The day dragged on and they were all lost in silence for most of it. Lisa and Emily tried to play cards but the rocking boat made it difficult and after one game of go fish, they gave up. The hardest part was not knowing how far they had come or where they were. The storm could have sent them north towards Vancouver Island or it could have sent them south back towards southern Washington or California. The worst case scenario was that the storm had sent them west and further from land.

It was late afternoon and after another boring meal of beef jerky and water everyone except Lisa, who was rowing again, had laid down to sleep. She was the only one who had slept the night before and they needed to rest. Emily was dozing. She was in that place between awake and full sleep when Lisa yelled out. Emily's gritty eyes popped open and she pushed herself up and frantically looked around. David and Mason had sat up as well and they were looking around in confusion. Lisa was paddling hard and her face was a mask of determination.

"What's wrong, Lisa? Why did you yell?" Emily asked her in bewilderment.

Lisa didn't even look at her. She just grunted out, "Boat!" in between heaving breaths.

Emily and the others scrambled up onto their knees and scanned the way ahead. It was Mason that spotted it.

"There! It's right there!" He pointed towards a dark shape ahead of them. David slid over to the emergency kit that had come with the boat and searched through it until he found the small pair of binoculars. Turning back, he scanned ahead again and cautioned,

"It could just be another dead boat guys. But even if it is we might be able to scavenge stuff from it."

Everyone waited impatiently while he looked through the glasses. It seemed to take forever before he lowered them and smiled. "There are people on deck! It looks like they are fishing."

He handed the glasses to Emily who was closest and she quickly brought them up to her eyes. When she had found the boat she squinted to make out two people who looked like they were hauling a net over the side. A sense of panic over took her and she almost threw the glasses at Mason as she dived for the other paddle. She shoved it at David.

"Quick! We need to get closer before they leave. It's late afternoon and it looked like they were hauling in nets. They might be done for the day. You're stronger than me so paddle, please!" David's eyes widened in understanding and he quickly moved to the side and got into position. Emily sat on her knees in the middle of the boat with her eyes locked on the fishing boat in the distance. She chanted a mantra in her head over and over, "Please stay, please stay..."

Mason went to try and take over for Lisa but she just shook her head and kept paddling. He watched her in admiration for a minute before turning to the emergency kit that David had left open. From the corner of her eye, Emily saw him remove something and her whole body jolted away from him. Mason was holding a gun. She slapped at her pockets and remembered in a flash that she had put Mark's gun in the bottom of her backpack. A whimper of fear escaped her.

Mason looked at her terror filled face with shock and quickly looked down at the gun in his hand. "Emily! Emily, it's a flare gun! We can signal them!" He tried to explain.

When her frozen brain finally understood what he was saying, she fell back onto her butt and dropped her head in to her hands. When she felt Mason put a hand on her shoulder, she looked up into his sad eyes.

"I'm sorry. I'm so sorry, Mason. I just flashed to Mark when I saw the gun in your hands," she whispered.

He shook his head in disbelief. "I would never hurt you or the others. I know you don't trust me but please know that."

The hurt in his eyes sent shame flooding through Emily. As he turned away she grabbed his wrist.

"I know you wouldn't, Mason. I really do! It's just that in the past three days, I've had two people point a gun at me and I panicked. Honestly, it wasn't you. It was the gun!" she pleaded with him to understand.

He searched her face for a moment before nodding and squeezing her hand in understanding. Then his face went fierce. "I will protect you. No one will hurt us again!"

He turned away before she could respond and all she could think was, "Wow". She glanced towards David and he gave her a quick nod before focusing back on his paddling.

Emily grabbed the binoculars and looked at the boat ahead of them. She could see that they were on the other side of the boat now, pulling up a different net. It wouldn't take long before they were done and if she guessed right they would leave. She wanted to scream in frustration at how long it was taking to get closer. They had to signal them but they had to do it when the people were looking so it wouldn't be missed.

"Get ready, Mason. When I see one of them turn this way you need to shoot the flare," she told him.

"Just say the word. I'm ready!"

Through the glasses, Emily watched as the people pulled the fishing net on board. The sun shone off the silver fish that spilled over the edge of the boat and disappeared onto the deck. She barely let herself breathe while waiting for one of them to turn. When it finally happened, Emily almost fell backwards. It seemed from a distance that the man who turned around was looking straight at her. She yelled, "NOW!" and jumped when Mason fired the flare. Her eyes followed the flare as it zoomed up over their heads and then she quickly brought the glasses up and looked to the boat to see if they had seen it. After finding the focus again, she found herself looking at two people that were waving their arms above their heads. Emily couldn't quite make out their features but she thought it was a man and a woman. The person she thought was a man lowered his arms and moved away from the woman and disappeared.

"They see us, guys! I think they see us!" she told the others.

Lisa slumped back against the side of the boat and tried to catch her breath. David leaned back also and rested his paddle on his knees. He wiped the sweat and salt spray from his face with his sleeve before speaking.

"Do you think they will come and get us?" he panted.

Before Emily could answer, they saw the boat turn towards them.

"Here they come. Please let them be nice people!" she begged.

Emily closed her eyes at the thought of more misfortune finding them. She looked at her backpack and decided she would be ready for anything. Snagging it with her foot, she pulled it closer and dug deep into it until she felt the cool metal of the gun. She pulled it out and stuffed it into the pocket of her jacket. When she looked up, Mason was looking at her with a frown on his face. Emily nodded at the flare gun he was still holding.

"Are there more flares for that? It's not ideal but it could be used as a weapon."

He opened his mouth to say something before closing it and slowly nodded. He turned to the emergency kit and pulled out two more flares.

David looked at Lisa and told her "Keep that paddle with you. You've got a great swing. Don't hesitate if things go wrong."

Lisa gripped her paddle close to her chest and gave a sharp nod. The sound of the fishing boat's engine was getting louder and they all turned to watch it approach. Everyone in the lifeboat was struggling with their emotions. They were excited at the possibility of being rescued and wary of what kind of people might be on the fishing boat. Emily prayed that they would be decent and willing to help them get to shore. She hated that there was an automatic suspicion after what happened on the Lawless.

When the two boats were about fifty feet apart, the sounds of the engine changed as it reversed and slowed to come alongside the lifeboat. This close, Emily could clearly make out the features of the woman that was staring down at them from the deck. She was an older woman and Emily guessed her age to be in the sixties or early seventies. She had a kind but weathered face, like she had spent many years outdoors. The woman had a concerned expression on her face but as the distance closed it changed to one of astonishment. She turned away and Emily could clearly hear her yelling at the man.

"Luke! Luke, they're kids! There are four teenagers in that boat. Hurry up and help me get them on board."

She turned back and yelled over the side at them. "Just hold on! We'll get you out of there in a jiffy!" and she disappeared from view.

Emily looked to the others to gauge their reactions. They all seemed to relax slightly, but David looked a little apprehensive still.

"I think they are okay but just stay sharp." He reached over and started to gather up things that were loose and stuffed them into the closest backpack.

Mason nodded and emptied the emergency kit supplies into another pack. There were still a few clothes draped out to dry so Emily and Lisa folded them up and packed them away. It didn't take long before the fishing boat was alongside them and David used his paddle to manoeuvre the lifeboat down its side and under the ladder. He tied them off on it and shouldered his pack. Looking up he could see the woman staring down at him with concern. The man who must be Luke stuck his head over and waved David up the ladder. His face was weather-creased and brown with sun like the woman's and his eyes were also concerned.

David scrambled up the ladder and felt strong steady hands grip him as he came over the rail. He almost panicked and struck out at them until the grip changed to a pat on his back.

"There you go, young fella. You're safe on board now. Don't you worry; we'll get all you kids up here safe and sound," the man said in a gravelly voice. He turned away and peered over the side for a moment before reaching out and helping Lisa over the rail. Emily and Mason quickly followed and the kids grouped together on deck, watching the two strangers warily.

The woman scanned them each in turn and nodded to herself.

"Well, you all look healthy enough. You must not have been out there for too long. My names Joanna and that's my husband Luke. We were just headed back in when we saw your flare. Good thing too as the weather will be turning in a few hours and you kids would have been battered right hard in that little dinghy. Well, come on then, let's go get settled and you can tell us your story on the way." She waved them towards the cabin but none of them moved.

David stepped forward. "Ma'am, we just want to say thank you for picking us up but could you tell us where we are and where you are taking us? We haven't had the best experiences with people out here and we are a little nervous right now," he said seriously.

The woman's face made a comical "oh" expression before it turned thunderous. She looked at the two girls and then swung back to David.

"Did somebody hurt you kids?" she asked in outrage. Before David could respond she barrelled on. "Well, you don't have to worry about that on my boat! No sir, Luke and I will take care of you and see that you get to shore. Oh, you poor babies! Imagine that! In a disaster like this people should be coming together to help each other. Unbelievable!" She seemed to run out of steam then and when she took in the wide-eyed stares, she smiled reassuringly and said softly. "It really is okay. You're safe with us."

Emily felt tears come to her eyes. This woman was so much like her granny who would also go off on tirades. In an instant, she felt like a little kid again. After all they had been through; here was an adult that wanted to take care of them. She found herself pushing past David as the tears broke free and wasn't surprised at all that Joanna opened her arms and wrapped them around her in a comforting hug.

Chapter 20

After Lisa had gotten a motherly hug and the boys received back pats, they entered the cabin and settled in. Joanna quickly presented them with hot coffee and ham sandwiches. While the kids ate, she filled them in on what had been happening on land.

"We were lucky. We live on an island named Samish and it only has a narrow landbridge to the mainland. There are only about five hundred houses on the island and half of those aren't full time residents. Most of us are already self-sufficient with generators and gardens. There isn't a big commercial presence on the island so we are used to fending for ourselves. The mainland wasn't so lucky. We could see the fires and smoke for days. Our youngest son made it home to us on day four and he told us of horrible things. So many people died on the first day from accidents and crashes. He told us that by day three people were rioting at stores and there was chaos everywhere. We barricaded the landbridge and posted guards but we couldn't just turn away families who were trying to find a safe place for their kids. We set up the community camp ground as a refugee center and we've just started to move people into empty homes. There's plenty of food to be had as long as you like seafood. Almost all the locals have knowledge of fishing, crabbing and clamming so no one will starve. Luke used to fish for a living on this old beast and he only retired from it a few years ago. This warhorse was old enough not to be affected by the pulse so we've been hauling in fish for the past ten days. It helps that we have an ice plant onboard so we can store the fish and pack it to transport it. We have about twelve working vehicles on the island and we have set up a delivery system to help some of the refugee camps on the mainland. I'm sorry to say that we have to send armed guards with them after they were attacked by starving people." When she paused to shake her head sadly, David jumped in.

"Where are we? We were caught in a storm last night and blown all over the place."

Joanna stood and peered out of the window and then waved them over. She pointed out to the north east.

"You can just see it now. That's Vancouver Island. We are headed into the Strait of Juan de Fuca. Samish Island is just northwest of Burlington and Mount Vernon."

David's expression was hopeful when he asked, "How far is that to the Canadian border?"

Joanna was surprised by the question. "Well, it's probably about sixty miles or so up the interstate. Why do you ask? Are you kids from B.C.?"

Wide grins had spread out on all the kids face's at her answer. They had made it so close to their home country that hope swelled in them all. Emily answered Joanna.

"No, we are from central Alberta."

"Alberta! Then how and the heck did you kids end up in the Pacific Ocean?"

Emily explained about the class trip to Disneyland and how they had found their way to the coast and onto the Lawless. Joanna was shocked at how far they had come.

"Well, that's just incredible! What are the odds of that! You know, you kids are so lucky. Luke and I have no reason to even be out here. There's plenty of fish closer to the Island. The only reason we came out into open water was to look for friends of ours. They had gone out the day before the pulse for a family getaway in their new cruiser. We were hoping to spot them adrift out here. We are so worried about them. Their two kids are like grandchildren to us."

The silence from the kids and the looks they sent each other confused Joanna.

"What? What's wrong?"

No one wanted to say what they were thinking but Lisa spoke up.

"The kids, they wouldn't be named Sarah and Ben would they?"

The shock on Joanna's face said it all. Lisa shook her head and let out a bitter laugh. "You don't have to worry about them. They are probably home by now!" she said sarcastically.

"What, you met them? How…what?" Joanna stuttered out in confusion.

Lisa just shook her head and looked away. Joanna was looking from face to face in bafflement. Emily sighed and explained.

"They took our boat or rather their father did. We stopped to help them and he had a shotgun and he ordered us off the boat and took it," she said quietly.

"Now that's a load of bull! There is no way Jacob would do that! Besides, I thought you said you were in a storm." Her face held disbelief and anger.

David intervened. "We were in the lifeboat when we were caught in the storm. Before that, when we had the boat, we stopped when we saw the children on deck. We offered to help them but the father was scared. He told us that another boat had stopped and stolen all their food and water…they took his wife. He was desperate and scared. He said he couldn't take the chance with us. He just wanted to protect his kids. He wanted us to go onto his boat but we convinced him to let us take the life boat so we would have a better chance of making it to shore." David paused as Joanna deflated and slumped down into a chair. "I think he was crazy with grief and desperation to protect his kids. I got the feeling he wasn't happy with what he did." David tried to console her.

Joanna just sat there shaking her head in disbelief. After a while she looked up at them. "I'm sorry. I'm sorry for what he did but you are all safe now and in a few hours we will be back on land and I will do whatever I can to help you kids make it home." She gave them all a sad smile and left the cabin.

The next two hours were mostly spent in silence. They were all exhausted and they dozed off one by one. Emily found herself nodding off only to jerk away with thoughts of home. It had been more than two weeks since they had last stood on land, the day the whole world had changed. On one hand, she wanted desperately to get to shore so they could continue their way home. But on the other, she was scared of leaving the ocean. Even after all the terrible things that had happened, they were somewhat sheltered from the reality that awaited them on land. She gave up trying to sleep and quietly left the cabin so as to not wake her friends.

She went to the bow and took a long look around. The sight that greeted her made her gasp. They were surrounded by land. She could see many small and large islands and mountains in the distance. They were almost to shore. Emily closed her eyes and tried to picture the area they were heading to on the map that they had studied. From what she remembered, they would come ashore south of Bellingham. She knew that was a small city a lot of Canadians crossed the border to shop at so it couldn't be too far from Canada. She opened her eyes with a sigh. With only their feet to travel on, everywhere would be far.

Joanna came up to the rail beside her. The older woman didn't speak at first just stared out at the view. When she finally spoke, it was with great sadness.

"So much death and destruction, the world will never recover to what it once was." She turned to Emily with such sorrow in her eyes that the girl couldn't help but reach out and take her hand.

"Jacob and Claire are good people. They are like family to us. I just can't believe she is gone and that he did the things you said he did." Joanna wiped a tear from her face.

Emily squeezed her hand. "I think that a lot of people are making bad choices for good reasons. We are all going to have to find a balance in this new world. The rules have changed and we will have to do what it takes to survive. We just have to be careful that we don't lose our humanity along the way. I honestly don't know what I would have done in Jacob's place. He had watched his wife being kidnapped and his kids starve. If I was him, I might have done the same thing. I just don't know. What I do know is that he didn't physically hurt us and he could have. What I also know is that he was a good enough man that you risked yourselves to try and find him and that led to you rescuing us. That is too much of a coincidence for me.

There is something or someone watching over us and whatever it was, it just steered things."

Joanna smiled down at Emily and pulled her into a loose hug. "You're awfully young to be so wise." They stood watching the small islands go by until Joanna pointed a head of them. "There it is, home! You should go get your friends."

Once everyone was on deck, Joanna pointed out features of her island home as they passed. She explained what was going to happen.

"We are going to drop you kids off at the campground. They have it set up for refugees. There are cabins and a first aid and food station. They will get you guys settled and you can relax for tonight. Luke and I need to unload this beast and then I will find out when there will be another shipment sent out. You kids can catch a ride with them to get you closer to the border. I'll come around in the morning to check on you and we'll make some plans." She gave them a reassuring smile before pointing at the shore. "That's our house!"

They all looked at the pretty home overlooking the water. The raised beds around the house were full of blooming spring flowers. As the house slowly slid past, they could see a man come around the side and start waving at them.

"That's my son, Will." She beamed and waved back. Will waved both arms over his head and pointed in the direction they were going. They all looked ahead and there was silence at what they saw. The nearest house to Joanna's also overlooked the water and sitting at the home's dock was the Lawless. Joanna's face was filled with relief that her friends had made it home but it quickly turned to determination when she looked at the kids and their blank expressions.

"All right then! I want you kids to know that we are going to make it up to you. What Jacob did was flat out wrong and I'll see to it that there is payment made. We will do everything in our power to get you guys home. You leave it with me and I'll take care of it!"

Emily smiled and David shook his head.

"Ma'am, thank you but we made it and I'm happy that those children are safe."

She just smiled and Emily knew from the look in her eyes she was planning something. It didn't take much longer before they were pulling in at another dock. Emily could see people gathered further up on shore and there were a few men walking on the beach with shotguns and rifles. She shot a nervous look at Joanna and the older woman waved at the closest one.

"You don't need to worry about them, sweetie. There have been a few boats that have come over from the mainland full of people who thought it would be better to take than receive so we patrol the beaches now. Anyone who comes looking for help is welcome but we are ready for anyone who is unfriendly. You kids can sleep soundly tonight." Joanna shot them a reassuring smile and move to help tie off the boat to the deck.

Luke came out on deck carrying a crate that was full of ice packed fish and stacked it by the ladder. David immediately went over to help and the two quickly stacked three more crates to be offloaded. They handed down the crates to men who had come out to help. Once they were done, Luke looked over at the group of teens that he had rescued and gave a brief nod before returning to the cabin.

Joanna smile at his back and rolled her eyes. "Don't mind, Mr. Chatty, he's not much for words but he's got a big heart. Okay! Let's get you kids onto solid ground. Grab your stuff and climb down onto the dock. I'll walk you up to the camp and introduce you to Betty. She's the one who organized everything and is running the camp."

Emily slung her pack over her shoulders and took a deep breath. "Here we go," she thought, and for the first time in over two weeks, she climbed down onto land. The others were quick to follow and Joanna led them up the gentle slope into the camp.

Emily found herself trying to look everywhere at once. There were groups of people sitting at picnic tables and others who were walking in between the cabins. There were children racing around in a game of tag and the sounds of their laughter calmed Emily's racing heart. She could see four women hanging clean laundry on clotheslines that were stretched between trees and others that were sorting items from a stack of boxes. As they drew closer to the main building, the trees opened up and there was a huge cleared area that was being worked on by many people. Some people were tilling the land and others were planting seeds. It was a beautiful sight to Emily and she ached for the chance to be home doing the same.

When they finally arrived at the main camp building, there were long tables set up with various foods spread over them. Three men and two women were chopping and slicing vegetables. On a table further away there was a man and woman working on the freshly delivered fish. At the main table a woman in her mid-forties looked up from her chopping and frowned at the group of teenagers heading her way. When she caught sight of Joanna her whole expression changed to relief. She came hurrying around the table and caught Joanna up in a hug.

"You're back! Thank goodness, I was so worried." She pulled back and stared closely at Joanna's face. "Did you find any sign of them?" the woman asked hopefully.

Joanna looked over at the teens before turning back and answering her. "We think he made it back with the children. It's…a long story. Betty, this is Emily, David, Lisa and Mason. We found them in a lifeboat out in the open water. Can you set them up in a cabin tonight? I want to head over to Jacob's place and see them."

Betty looked confused by Joanna's answer about their neighbour but quickly nodded and smiled in welcome at the kids. "Of course! Welcome to Samish Island. If you will come with me, I will show you to an empty cabin and fill you in on what's happening here."

As she stepped away from them, Joanna gave them another smile and said,

"I'll be back in the morning after breakfast and we will discuss how to get you kids home. Enjoy supper and have a good sleep."

They all stood watching as Joanna went back down the hill towards the old fishing boat. After a few minutes, Betty ushered them away and they followed her to a small wooden cabin with a pretty little front railed porch. Betty went in first and started to open windows to air it out. The cabin was small with two rooms. The main room had a worn sofa and arm chair that faced a field stone fire place. Under the front window was a tiny dinette with four chairs. The bedroom had a double bed and a set of bunk beds against one wall. The room also had the smallest closet that Emily had ever seen. Once the tour was over they stood in the main room facing Betty.

"There are outhouses just behind the cabin and buckets by the water pump over at the main building so you can bring water over for washing up. The main building has working toilets and showers are available in the mornings and in the evenings. There's a sign-up sheet on the wall by the washroom doors for that. Dinner is at six tonight and breakfast is at seven. Lunch is very small and cold, usually just a sandwich and piece of fruit. Once I show you boys to your cabin, you can get cleaned up and we will all meet for supper. We can discuss what work skills you have and where you will be working in the future."

When Betty took a breath to go on, David interrupted her.

"Thank you, ma'am, we appreciate you letting us stay tonight and the hot supper is a real treat but we will be heading on in the morning after we talk to Joanna. Also, we would be much more comfortable staying together in one cabin."

Betty's face creased into a huge frown. "Young man, it's not proper for you two boys to be spending the night in the same room as these girls. The world out there is in chaos. It's no place for children to be running around. It would be wrong of me to let you leave here where it's safe and protected."

This time it was Emily that interrupted her.

"Thank you again for your hospitality. We will get our things and leave now." She stared the woman down with deadly serious eyes.

Betty sputtered, "You have no idea what's out there!"

Emily tilted her head and said with the same dead serious tone, "We were at Disneyland...California when it happened. We know what's out there because we walked through it. We have spent every night together since this all began and we will continue together until we make it home."

When Betty just stood there in shock, Emily continued. "May we please stay together tonight in this cabin? After we speak with Joanna in the morning, we will be heading out. Our parents and families are waiting for us."

Betty finally nodded. "I...yes, of course. I'm sorry. I didn't know you had come so far. I...well. I'll leave you to get cleaned up and will see you in twenty minutes at supper." She hurried out of the cabin and softly closed the door.

Emily slumped down on the worn sofa. She was suddenly drained and all she wanted to do was sleep. Lisa sat down beside her and leaned against her. It was comforting in a way. Mason sat on the arm chair and tilted his head back before closing his eyes. David wandered around the room for a minute before leaving the cabin. They were all so tired that they dozed off.

David woke them up ten minutes later when he came back with a bucket full of water and a bar of soap. Emily felt drugged as she washed her hands and face and then followed the others out of the cabin and over to the main building. As twilight fell, there were people lighting torches along the pathways. The doors of the main building were propped open and the bright light of electricity flooded out. The combination of light and amazing cooking smells perked Emily up. They went in and joined the line that was edging towards a simple buffet. There was a huge pot of soup as the main meal but it was the small plates of greens that caught Emily's attention. It had been so long since she had had anything fresh that she felt her mouth water at the plates of salad with chunks of tomatoes on top. There were pans with fried fish and small glasses of juice as well. David let out a whoop of excitement when he spotted the tray with tiny oatmeal cookies and the woman behind the table laughed at his expression and handed him an extra.

They picked a table away from the main part of room and dug in to their simple but filling meal. Once the edge of her hunger was sated, Emily let her eyes roam around the room and took in all the other people that were dining. Most seemed to be content but there were a few that looked shell shocked and overwhelmed. The one thing they all had in common was that they all looked clean. Emily scratched at her itchy head. Her hair was brittle from the salt water and her clothes were stiff. David noticed her fingering her hair and smiled.

"When I came over earlier to get the water bucket, I put all of our names down for showers tonight. There are a few people ahead of us but it shouldn't be too long of a wait. There's a tray by the door that has little paper cups filled with soap and shampoo. I can't wait to get this salt crust off of me."

Emily and Lisa beamed happily at him and Mason nodded with a smile. They finished up their food and took their empty trays back to the dishwashers. The thought of being clean sent them straight back to the cabin and they all grabbed their one extra change of clothes. Emily made a note to herself to see about washing their salt encrusted clothes before they moved on. When they arrived at the shower room doors there were only four people waiting in line. The two men and two women waiting there stared at the kids before turning their backs. David raised his eyebrows in a question at the others but they just shrugged. Emily didn't care. She just wanted to be clean and then sleep. The camp was a nice setup but she wanted to be home and she wasn't looking to make friends. Once it was their turn, they all took the little cups of soap and separated into the men's and women's rooms. The hot water felt like heaven and if there had been more shampoo available, Emily would have scrubbed her hair a second time. As she pulled on her clean clothes, she felt sluggish and drowsy. The hot meal and hot shower had sapped all her strength as the lack of sleep from the past few days caught up to her. Lisa had to steer her back to the cabin and she helped her into bed. As Emily closed her eyes, she had a small smile on her face. Next step…home.

Chapter 21

In the morning, Emily woke with a sense of excitement. Even though they had travelled hundreds of miles by boat, it didn't feel like they had. Today they would start the final leg of their journey home and she was itching to start walking. Everyone else must have felt the same because they were up early and ready to go. The main building was set up for breakfast and they eagerly joined the line that was forming. The meal was once again simple but filling. There was the biggest pot Emily had ever seen filled with oatmeal and raisins. A few bowls filled with canned fruit and small glasses of juice were also available. The teens savoured the meal as they knew that it would be the last one they had before they had to cook over a campfire.

After they had finished their meal they headed back to the cabin and packed their bags. Emily was getting antsy to leave but there was no sign of Joanna. They had gathered on the front porch with their bags ready at their feet. Emily was pacing back and forth ready to be on the way. They had just started talking about getting directions and leaving when they heard the sound of engines heading their way. They all turned to look around, trying to spot where the noise was coming from. It wasn't long before two ATVs and one Quad came towards them from the main road leaving the camp. Joanna was leading them and Emily could see the two other riders where men. As they got closer she saw David stiffen and Lisa gasped. As the riders got closer, Emily realized that one of the riders was Jacob, the man who had stolen their boat.

When the three riders pulled up to the cabin and stopped, the teens were all on their feet on the porch staring down at them with grim silence. Jacob looked them over quickly and then stared at the ground. The other man with them was in his early thirties and he stared at them with a scowl on his face. Joanna approached the cabin and smiled.

"Good morning! I hope you all had a good night. This is my son Will and you know Jacob. We have some ideas about helping you kids get home. Jacob?" She turned and waved him forward.

Jacob didn't seem like he was going to speak or even look at them for a minute. Emily was about to say something when he finally reached up and rubbed his forehead. He took a step forward and raised his eyes to them.

"What I did to you kids…" He stopped and shook his head and cleared his throat. "What I did was wrong and I'm sorry. I was out of my head with grief for my wife and desperation for my children. I'm sorry and I'd like to try and make it up to you." He lowered his head again and Emily clearly saw the regret in his eyes.

It was David that replied to him. "Sir, we are sorry for what happened to your family. I'm glad you got your kids to safety. We would appreciate any help you could give us to get home."

Emily shot a quick look at Mason who was frowning and Lisa who stood with a blank face. She hoped they wouldn't say anything. There was no point in rehashing what had happened and if these people were willing to help them get closer to home they should just let it go. Jacob nodded at Joanna and her son crossed his arms and looked away angrily. Emily couldn't tell who he was mad at.

Joanna sent Jacob a compassionate smile and turned to the teens.

"All right then. Will is leaving tomorrow to make a fish delivery to some of the rescue camps set upon the mainland. They go with armed guards and we think you should go with them. Their route will take you to about thirty miles from the Canadian border and past some of the more dangerous areas. Luke, my husband, and I talked it over and we want to give you kids this ATV. Jacob is going to give you his. You can double up on them and make much better time. Gas will be easy to find with all the abandoned cars on the roads. You just need to siphon it. We will give you some extra food and water and with a little luck, it should only take you about a week to get home."

Emily was shocked by the generous offering and she saw her friends felt the same. Mason's face had a huge grin on it and Lisa had closed her eyes in relief. David had walked down the steps with his hand out to Jacob.

"Sir, we can't thank you enough!" he said as he shook the hand of the now smiling man. When he tried to shake Joanna's son's hand, the man angrily waved him off and sent a glare at his mother. Emily saw this over Joanna's shoulder as she hugged the woman in gratitude. She pulled back from her and her smile changed to concern.

Joanna looked behind her and met the glare of her son. He opened his mouth to speak but she beat him to it.

"Not one word! For the last time, this is not your decision to make!" she snapped at him harshly. Will shut his mouth and turned and walked away.

Joanna took a deep breath and turned back to the kids. "He's not happy with giving up the ATVs but we have an extra one and a truck that still works. It's more than most people have and it's the right thing to do. Don't worry about him. He'll get over it." Joanna smiled reassuringly at them before continuing. "You kids just relax for today and I'll be back at dawn to get you. Be ready because they like to get on the road as soon as possible. I'll head over and let Betty know that you'll be staying another night." Joanna called her son back over and Jacob gave them a nod before they started up their machines and rode away.

David slung his arm around Emily's shoulder as they watched them leave. "This is huge, Emily. We will be home in no time now. I figured on at least two or three weeks walking to get there but with ATVs it will only be days."

Emily smiled up at him. His face was so full of hope and happiness. She was happy too but she couldn't get the angry look on Will's face out of her mind. They would be leaving with him in the morning and she hoped he had a change of heart by then.

"I'm going to grab Lisa and see about washing up our clothes. Everything is still covered in salt and it would be nice to clean them while we can."

"Good idea! Would you mind doing mine as well? I want to go around and see if anyone is familiar with what's between here and the border. It would be good to know what we are facing before we get there," he said.

"Yes, of course. We might as well do Mason's clothes too but you boys are doing the next load!" she teased him.

Lisa and Emily unpacked their bags and sorted out the salt encrusted clothes. Once they had the boys' laundry, they headed to the main building to see what the setup was. They were directed to a fire pit off to the side of the building that had a big barrel of water over it. There were tin washtubs and plastic containers set up in a row. Emily was delighted to see an antique roller wringer on a stand. After washing and rinsing the clothing they took turns feeding each piece through the wringer while the other cranked the handle. There were clotheslines strung between trees and they hung everything to dry in the spring sun.

When they got back to the cabin, David and Mason were gone. She puttered around the small room but couldn't seem to settle. Lisa was staring out the window with a far off look on her face. Emily knew her friend was still trying to deal with what happened on the boat with Mark. She wished that she could help but knew that Lisa would have to come to terms with it herself. She gave the girl a hug and reminded her that she was there for her if she wanted to talk but Lisa just sadly shook her head.

"I'm going to go for a walk and see what else is around here. Are you sure you don't want to come?"

"Thanks, Emily, but I just need to have some time to think. Thank you for being such a good friend. It means more to me than you will ever know."

After another quick hug, Emily slipped out of the cabin. She needed something to occupy herself or she would go crazy waiting to leave in the morning. She saw people carrying boxes and crates into the main building and decided to head over and see if she could help out with anything. When she poked her head in the main doors, she saw that all the tables were empty but she heard voices coming from the kitchen area. When she saw Betty walking by the door, she headed that way. The kitchen was bustling with people prepping for the next meal and when she caught Betty's eye, she went over to the lady.

"Excuse me, ma'am. I was hoping you could put me to work. I'm pretty good in the kitchen but I could lend a hand with whatever needs doing."

Betty wiped her hands on a towel and smiled at her. "We can always use extra hands around here. It's Emily, right? Follow me and I'll introduce you to these busy ladies. They'll love the extra help!"

Emily spent the rest of the day hard at work with her mind occupied. They all chatted as they made up sandwiches for lunch and prepped the food that would go into dinner. Her heart felt light in the warm room. It was so much like being at home during the holidays when her mom and all her aunts would work together to prepare the holiday meal. At one point, she felt tears dripping down her face in homesickness. The woman next to her handed her a dish towel and rubbed her back.

"Don't worry, sweetie. I do that at least three times a day."

She worked all day helping to make food and clean and wash dishes. When the dinner was being served, Betty handed her a tray and told her to go and eat. She offered to stay and wash dishes but the older woman just shooed her out.

"Go on now, eat with your friends. You've done enough today and Joanna says you will be leaving at dawn. I put your name down on the evening shower list. You've got a long road ahead of you so take what comforts you can before you leave."

Emily impulsively threw her arms around Betty. "Thank you for letting me help out today and for everything else you have done for us. I won't forget you!"

Betty smiled and nodded then pushed Emily towards the dining area where her friends were waiting. When she settled at their table they were talking about tomorrow and what David and Mason had learned from some of the others in the camp.

David was talking about the border crossing. "They said that they tried to cross into B.C. because they have family in the interior but that guards have the border crossings locked down. They aren't letting anyone across even with Canadian ID. Other people that know that area said it was just a chain link fence and if you go further away from the crossing there would be no one to stop us from just going over it. They said there isn't even a fence in some places. We shouldn't have a problem. With the ATVs, we don't even have to stay on the roads. We can easily go over fields if we have to." He looked at all of them and grinned. "We will be in Canada tomorrow night!"

They finished their dinners and stacked their trays in the dish area before heading back to the cabin. Emily was happy to see the neat pile of clothing that Lisa had taken down from the lines and folded. After they had repacked their backpacks, they headed to the showers. They all knew that it would probably be the last one they had for a very long time.

Lying in bed, Emily stared at the ceiling and thought about Alex. Where was she? How far had they come and were they all still alive? Her biggest hope after seeing her parents were that Alex and her other friends would already be home or that they would arrive soon after.

Chapter 22

The night was barely lightened in the east when Emily and her friends filed out of the cabin and stood on the front porch. The outline of a person was walking towards them from the main road. Emily felt a surge of apprehension. For some reason she felt that things were not going to go by the plan. She let out the breath she didn't know she was holding when Joanna stepped into the torchlight and she was smiling in greeting.

"Good morning! I see you are all ready to go. Follow me. The trucks are waiting out on the main road." She turned back the way she had come and they followed her out of the campground. Waiting on the road were three old pickup trucks and seven different ATVs and Quads. Two of them had supplies strapped to the back but were riderless. Joanna walked them over to them and waved her son, Will, to join them. He was still clearly upset by his Mother's decision but he didn't say anything.

"I want you to stay between the trucks at all times. The men will be on guard and they all have weapons. Stay with them until they get to the last drop off and then William will show you the way to go from there. You should try and stay off the interstate. There are a lot of desperate people out there that would kill you for what you have." She paused and looked at each one of them before continuing. "I will pray that you get home safely. Good luck." Joanna pulled Will into a tight embrace and spoke softly to him. When they separated, she smiled at the kids again and turned to walk away.

Emily called out to her. "Thank you, Joanna! Thank you for saving us!"

Will stared at her for a moment before barking out at them.

"Load up! Stay between the trucks and keep your mouths shut. Once we get to the mainland, anything or anyone could be waiting for us. We need to stay sharp and we can't be babysitting you bunch." He practically snarled the last sentence before turning away. Emily saw Mason's face darken in anger and she quickly grabbed his arm and shook her head. There was no point in fighting with the jerk. In a few hours, they would be away from him and on their way alone.

David, Mason and Emily were all experienced riders but they had decided to let the boys drive for the first leg. Once they were on and settled, Emily climbed on behind Mason and Lisa joined David. Lisa had made peace with Mason over their past but she was still uncomfortable being too close to him.

They stayed tucked between the first and second truck. It was still too dark to see any of the scenery so Emily spent the first hour with her head tucked down behind Mason's back. By the time the sun was up and it was bright enough to see, they had crossed the landbridge and were on the mainland. Emily didn't know what she expected to see but everything looked fairly normal. There were all types of vehicles that had been pushed off to the side of the road, but that was the only thing out of place. As they got closer to the first town that they would drive through, there were more signs of destruction. Some of the homes were boarded up and had smoke coming out of the chimneys but others had windows smashed out and doors hanging open. There was a block that they drove by that all the houses had burned to the ground. The strangest sight to Emily was a long stretch of road that had every car wide open. Front and back doors and trunks were all open. What she didn't see was people. No one was out walking around and that coupled with the silence made her shiver.

As they went through the main business district, the damage was much more prevalent. Stores and restaurants had been looted heavily and there weren't any windows left intact. She was saddened by all the damage around her and then baffled. For some reason, someone had pulled down the golden arches of a McDonald's sign and it hung from its pole by wires. Shaking her head at the senselessness of it, she heard her belly rumble and images of the restaurant's famous breakfast came to mind. She groaned at the knowledge that there might never be another one made. A sudden anger came over her. Who had done this? Who had caused the misery all around them? They had been so focused on getting home that none of her friends had even asked that question. They only had what Emily had seen on CNN the day everything stopped to go by. Did anyone even know who had done this terrible thing? At this point, did it even matter?

A shout from ahead pulled her from her dark thoughts and she felt the ATV slow before coming to a stop. With the big truck in front of them she couldn't see what was happening but a look at the relaxed guards told her everything was fine. They were moving again in minutes and they passed through an open gate. Chain link fence surrounded a building that Emily recognized as a large hotel. The guards jumped from their machines and dropped the tailgate of the truck that they had been following. David quickly jumped in to help when he saw that they were unloading the boxes and crates and carrying them inside. Will scowled at him but didn't say anything when David lifted a crate and followed the others. Emily nudged Mason and he joined in as well.

The men made quick work of the unloading and they were heading back through the gate within twenty minutes. Emily was happy when they left the damaged town and got back into the countryside. It was easier to look at the new spring growth on trees and in fields than the destroyed town. That thought ended when she started to see people walking along the sides of the road. They were like zombies. Whole families would stop and stare at them as they drove by with empty eyes. They were filthy and ragged and way too thin. Emily had to sob when they passed a mother and father with their two small children. The mother was holding a toddler and it looked like it was dead. The father held the hand of a little girl in a ragged pink dress and when they passed them she waved her stick thin arm like it was a parade. Mason reached down and squeezed her arm that was around his waist but they didn't stop. She wanted to scream at the guards to do something, anything to help, but their blank faces told her that they wouldn't.

The next time she looked to the side of the road, they were passing a pile of bodies. They had been thrown in a heap like garbage. After that sight, she couldn't take anymore so she tucked her head down behind Mason's back and stayed that way until they came to the next stop. Emily didn't even look up when Mason left her to help unload. She couldn't face any more of the horror in this new world. Then they were moving again and she tried to distract her broken mind with all the things her parents would have done in the last few weeks.

They had plenty of food in the cellar and with the chickens and cows food would not be an issue, at least not right away. She tried to remember if there was anyone in their area who had older farm equipment. She knew that Quinn's grandparents had a few antiques that they displayed at farm fairs so they most likely would have started tilling and planting some of the fields. It was too soon to plant the garden where they lived and it was possible that there had even been a final snow. She could picture all her neighbours gathering for a meeting to plan for getting the fields planted. Her mother's face popped in to her head and Emily could imagine the worry lines between her eyes deepening as she tried to come to terms with her only child's fate. "I'm coming, mom. I'm coming!" she whispered softly.

The ATV slowed for a third time and Emily straightened her shoulders. This was it. They would be leaving the convoy and heading out on their own after this. After the men had unloaded the final truck, this time into a huge community center, they went back out the gate and drove on for another twenty minutes. When they finally stopped they were away from any buildings and there were trees and fields all around them. The guards all dismounted and stood around them. Will came out of the lead truck and walked back towards them. He scanned their faces and firmed his mouth.

"Alright, this is as far as we go. Grab your stuff and as much of the supplies as you can carry." He told them in an even tone.

Mason, David and Lisa looked at each other in confusion but Emily just stared right at him. David was the first to speak.

"What are you talking about? Why do we have to carry the supplies?"

Will didn't answer him. He just stared him down with cold resolve. Emily pulled herself from behind Mason and grabbed a pack. As she started to pull things off the back of the machine, she answered David for him.

"He's not letting us take the ATVs. He was never going to let us go with them."

Her voice was flat. She had somehow known last night that this would happen. Once the ATV was unloaded, she looked up at David.

"Get your stuff, David. Once they are gone, we will try and spread it out amongst our packs."

She started to carry things over to the side of the road when Lisa grabbed her own pack and started to help her. Her friend's face was fierce but she didn't say anything and she didn't even look at the men that were waiting for them to finish.

David spun around and shouted at Will. "How can you do this? Your Mother was trying to help us! Jacob was trying to make up for what he did to us!"

Will said nothing. He just waited. Finally, with a yell of frustrated rage, David spun away and started to pull the supplies from the back of the machine that he had been riding. When they were finished, there was a large mound of backpacks and supplies sitting on the side of the road. Two of the men who had been passengers in the trucks jumped onto the machines and moved them back down the road. Will stepped forward and looked at the pile of supplies that his mother had given them and then looked at each one of them.

"There is no way you will be able to carry all of that. I'll take..." That's as far as he got before Emily stepped right up to him and yelled in to his face.

"YOU will take NOTHING! You went against her wishes with the ATVs but the supplies she gave us are ours! I will stand here and give this food to the starving people you and your men so callously drove past. Unlike YOU we are good decent people and WE will help others if we can! So if you want this food you will have to shoot me to get it!" She stood there with her chest heaving in a rage and met every one of the men's eyes until they looked down in shame. Emily seared Will with her anger until he too broke her stare and backed away.

"Load 'em up! I want to be home by supper," he called out to his men. None of them looked at the kids on the side of the road as they turned their trucks around and drove away.

Emily stared defiantly down the road until the sound of the engines faded. When David stepped up to her and put his hand on her arm, she turned and stared at him.

"Every time we find good people we get slapped with the bad. David...I...I just want to go home!"

"It's okay, Em. We'll get home. I promise. Come on - let's get this stuff sorted out," he told her.

She looked down at the pile of supplies and nodded. There was too much for them to carry but they could still take a lot of it. As they divided up the pile, Emily glanced at Lisa. She hadn't said anything but her face was tense and her eyes were filled with anger. Mason just looked lost. As he latched his pack and swung it onto his shoulder, Emily saw a glimpse of tears in his eyes. He would have to adjust. He had been handed almost everything in his life and now the harsh reality was that he would have to work for it all.

Once they had crammed as much as they could into the six backpacks, there was still a pile on the road. Emily hoped that it would help some poor family make it through another day. David spread the map open on the road and they all crowded around it. He pointed out their location and ran his finger north towards the border.

"We should get off this road. If we take side roads and cut across fields, we should have less of a chance of running into other people. I think we should head northeast. That way we can cross over the border somewhere here." He pointed out an area that had no towns or official crossing. "Walking is going to take longer but we should still be in Canada within three or four days. The last town we dropped supplies in was only forty miles south of the border. We just need to keep going."

He looked up at the others and everyone nodded so he folded the map and stood up. He grabbed one of the extra packs and Mason hauled the other one. They would have to take turns carrying them but the supplies were too precious to leave behind. No one spoke as they started north. They were still reeling from the betrayal of Joanna's son and soon they fell in to a rhythm. There was nothing to do but walk, one foot in front of the other, every step taking them closer to their country and home.

Chapter 23

The highway they were travelling on ran straight north to the town of Sumas. People in the campground had told them that the border guards weren't allowing anyone through so they took the first eastbound side road. They walked past fields that hadn't been planted and farm houses that had been boarded up. Twice they saw men with cold faces standing in their driveways with guns. They kept walking. When the road they were on bent to the south, they cut across fields until they found another road going east. The fields were soft with spring mud and they were all exhausted by the struggle to get through them. When they got back onto a road, they would stop and scrape the sticky mud from their pant legs and shoes. Emily felt like she was walking in concrete blocks instead of shoes when the mud dried. They eventually came to a forested area and entered the cool dimness on a game trail. The forest floor wasn't as muddy and they kept ploughing ahead.

Emily saw Lisa stagger over a root and called for a break. She had no idea how many miles they had walked but she knew that they all needed to rest and eat. Her best guess was that they still had three or four hours until dark. When she dropped her pack to the needle-covered floor, her shoulders ached from the unaccustomed strain the straps had caused. She was hungry and thirsty but she needed to just sit for a minute before addressing either need.

Looking at the others as they'd dropped down onto the forest floor, she could see that they were just as tired. It was to be expected. None of them had done any exercise in the last three weeks other than sitting on a boat and they all felt the pain in their muscles. Emily dragged her pack over and pulled out a bottle of water and two granola bars. They disappeared quickly into her hungry body and she added a strip of beef jerky to her meal. It wasn't the most satisfying food but it gave her flagging energy a boost and she knew in a few hours when they stopped to camp for the night, they would have a hot meal.

While they rested, there was no conversation. That suited her just fine. There was nothing to say. When David stood, the others did the same and they trudged on. After twenty minutes of navigating the trail, there was a crash of foliage ahead of them as some large animal fled through the forest. All four of them froze in their tracks and Lisa let out a frightened squeak. Emily saw a flash of tan as the deer they had startled fled deeper in to the forest away from the trail. They continued on, but it reminded Emily that bad people weren't the only thing they might have to worry about. Bears, cougars even wild pigs could be a danger to them if they stayed in the forest, and they would have to be on watch for them as well. She slid her hand into her jacket pocket and felt the cold hard metal of the gun. She had put it in there before they left the campground that morning and was reassured by its presence. It wouldn't stop a charging bear but it might help scare one off.

As much as Emily tried to stay focused on her surroundings, she found herself blanking out as she followed behind Lisa and David. Her eyes stayed on the floor of the forest to avoid tripping on the roots that covered the trail. It was two hours later when she walked right into Lisa's back. Quickly catching her balance, she looked up and saw the light had changed. They were at the edge of the woods that they had been travelling through. Emily moved up to stand by David and she looked at what was ahead of them. There was an unploughed field that ran all the way to a town in the distance. There were several fires burning and she counted eight smoke trails. They backed up further into the woods and tried to decide what to do.

David rubbed his face in exhaustion. "I think we should move further back into the trees and set up a camp. I don't know about you guys but I'm beat. The sun will be down in an hour and it would take longer than that to circle around that town. What do you guys think?" he asked.

Mason kicked at a root that was sticking out of the ground before answering, "Yeah, I think we're done for the day."

Lisa just nodded. Instead of replying, Emily moved back down the trail and started looking for a good place to set up camp. She found a decent clearing and dropped her pack. She asked Lisa to help her and they started searching for rocks. They collected enough to make a fire ring and she used a sharp edged stone to scoop out some dirt before going to search for small twigs and moss to help start the fire. While the girls got the fire ring arranged, the boys started to collect dry firewood. Emily let David start the fire as he had always been better at it than her. She pulled a pot and a pan from the backpacks and started to sort through the food. Emily didn't have a lot of energy left but she wanted a hot meal. Joanna had included powdered eggs, three tins of ham and a dozen potatoes in the supplies she had packed for them so that's what they had for supper. It was simple to prepare and cook and it filled them up.

After they had eaten, they washed the pan with as little water as possible and set the pot on the coals for hot water. As it was heating, she helped Lisa clear a spot for their blankets and had to dig up a few rocks that would have stabbed into them. They only had a few blankets from the boat and Joanna hadn't included any in what she had provided for them so Lisa and Emily were going to double up. With the water steaming, they used a wash cloth and cleaned themselves up as best they could before banking the fire and lying down for the night. The soft forest sounds and Lisa's warmth coupled with the long day helped Emily fall asleep despite the hard ground.

She felt like she had just closed her eyes when Mason's angry curses jerked her awake. There was a soft hazy grey light of dawn and she could see him stomping around. She sat up quickly and grasped the gun in her pocket while looking frantically around for the threat.

When she spotted David sitting with his head in his hands she relaxed slightly but still looked around in confusion. Lisa sat up and looked at Mason in annoyance.

"Mason! What is wrong with you? What's going on?" she snapped at him.

He swung around to stare at her and opened his mouth to answer but then shut it and walked over to a tree and kicked it. Emily looked at David who met her stare across the almost out fire. Before she could ask, he told her.

"We were robbed. Somebody came in while we were sleeping and stole our packs." he told her in a dead voice. She automatically reached down and flipped her and Lisa's ground sheet back. Relief flooded through her at the sight of the two packs they had used as pillows.

"Lisa and I still have ours!" she exclaimed.

David closed his eyes in relief for a moment before they flew open in anger. "Argggggg! I'm such an idiot! We should have never had a fire until it was dark. They would have seen the smoke and known right where to find us. What a stupid mistake!" He dropped his head in to his hands again.

Emily shook her head. It was a dumb mistake and so was not posting a watch. They were going to have to start being more careful if they had any chance of making it home. She pulled open her pack and dumped out the contents and did the same with Lisa's. Eight water bottles, six granola bars, four power bars, two small bags of rice four packages of ramen noodles, one bag of beef jerky and some multi vitamins was all the food they had. Two changes of clothes, two flashlights, some first aid, two tooth brushes, a stick of deodorant and a roll of toilet paper were all that was left for four people. They had lost almost everything.

Emily stood up and went over to pick up the pot and pan by the fire. She brought them back to her bag and started stuffing everything back in except for two water bottles. When she was done she handed one bottle to Lisa and one to Mason.

"Half for each of us, enjoy your breakfast."

She started to roll up the blankets and make a sling of them. She was on autopilot and didn't notice the others staring at her. When David said her name, she looked up and saw them all looking at her.

"What? People suck but they didn't kill us and there's nothing we can do so let's go." She stood and slung the blankets over her shoulder and across her chest.

Everyone was still standing and staring at her so she shook her head and started back to the trail. There was no point in dwelling on what they had lost. All they could do was keep moving. When she hit the trail, she stopped to wait and the others joined her in a few minutes. She looked to each one of her friends as they joined her and raised her eyebrows in a question. They all nodded determinedly so she fell in behind David and they headed north.

They had left their camp at dawn and walked for hours. They skirted the small town they had seen the previous day and kept going. She and Lisa passed the bottle of water back and forth taking small sips so that it lasted for two hours. The hunger she ignored. Emily knew that it was nothing more than a nuisance at this point. They had eaten well for the last twenty days and after seeing the starved people on the highway she knew her rumbling stomach didn't mean anything. Her biggest concern was water. They would have to get more and as their small supply of bleach was gone that meant boiling and filtering it. All of that would take time. As she followed along, she kept her mind focused on what steps they could take to get food.

When David slowed down and came to a stop, Emily guessed that they had been walking for six hours and it was somewhere around noon. He dropped the pack that he had been carrying and looked off into the distance. They were in a field and there was a house not far away. When he asked if they still had the binoculars, she could only shake her head.

With a grim expression, he squared his shoulders.

"Okay, you guys stay here and take a break. I think that house is empty and I'm going to go take a look. If it's abandoned, I'll come back and we can all go in and see if we can find some stuff to help us."

When no one objected, he turned and jogged towards the house. While they waited, Emily broke a power bar into three pieces and handed them out. The small amount of food only made her want more. David was back in less than ten minutes. He squatted down and took the small section of bar that Emily handed him. As he ate it, she pulled another bottle of water out and they all shared it.

When David finished his portion of the water, he told them what he had found.

"Both the doors are wide open and a couple of the windows have been busted. I didn't go in but it looks like no one's been there for a while. I think we should go check it out. At the least we might find some clothes for Mason and me."

Everyone got to their feet and followed David to the ransacked house. When they walked in the open front door and into the destroyed living room, Emily tried not to let it affect her. The place had been trashed and she carefully stepped over a family portrait that was lying in broken glass on the floor. She looked away quickly and tried to harden her heart but it was hard not to realize that this used to be a family's home. The kitchen was beyond bare. Whoever had come in here had ripped cabinet doors off and smashed all the dishes. She knew it was useless but she tried the kitchen faucets anyways. Nothing, they were bone dry. They all separated and started looking for anything they could use.

Emily wandered from room to room. She felt like a ghost. Is this what her home looked like? Had people came in to her family's home and ripped it apart? She went up the stairs and the first room she came to was done in shades of purple and pink. Stuffed bears had been thrown everywhere and posters of boy bands had been half ripped from the walls. An iPhone in a hot pink case caught her eye. It was half way tucked under the bed ruffle on the floor. She reached down to pick it up and saw that it was clipped to a dark purple school backpack that had been shoved under the bed. Emily sat on the bed and opened the zipper. It had a few binders and note books in it so she removed them and set them carefully on the night stand. In the bottom of the bag were three Mars bars and a package of jolly ranchers. She closed her eyes and thanked the girl for the calorie packed treats.

Emily left the room and went into the master bedroom down the hall. David and Mason were sorting through the pile of men's clothing on the bed so she went into the attached bathroom. It was a spa like setting with a huge sunken tub. There were bottles of lavender bath salts and creams on the side and she imagined sitting in a steaming tub of hot water filled with bubbles. With a sigh, she turned away and started to search through the cabinets. Two towels and a half roll of toilet paper went into her new empty pack. After digging around under the sink she came out with a half filled box of tampons and sighed in relief. Taking one last look around the room, she started to leave when something made her stop. Her forehead furrowed in concentration. What was she missing, something about the tub and a hot bath? When it came to her, her face broke out in a grin and she raced into the bedroom.

"David! We need to find the hot water tank. It should be filled with clean water!" She told him happily.

He smiled at her and started nodding. "Good thinking, Emily! Can you put these clothes in that pack? I'll go down into the basement and start looking for it. See if you can find some containers or plastic bottles we can use." He handed her the clothes he had picked up and left the room. Mason followed him with a confused look on his face.

When she got downstairs, Lisa was in the dining room and she had some things spread out on the table.

"Emily, I found a sleeping bag! It was in a garbage bag in the garage and look, this is lamp oil. We can use it to help start our campfires, right?"

"Good job, Lisa! That will definitely help."

They were in the house for almost an hour and they left with water, a few candy bars and a much better frame of mind. They walked all afternoon through fields and on roads where they could. Emily estimated that they had walked around twenty to twenty five miles that day when they finally stopped. They moved into a wooded area and crossed a stream before finding a cleared area where they set up camp. After two days of walking, they were all stiff and sore and starving. The stream that they had passed had given Emily an idea so while the water boiled on the small fire David had lit, she used the utility knife he had found at the house and started to cut and strip small green branches. She bent them into shape and used the bark strips to tie it all together. It was almost full dark so she used the flashlight to make her way back to the stream. She scanned the stream until she found a narrow spot and collected rocks. Placing her trap into the water she used the rocks to wedge it in tight and weigh it down. With any luck, they would have a fish for breakfast.

Lisa was fascinated by the trap and asked question after question on how to make one. Emily smiled over at David as she was remembering the summer that they had learned how to make one. Josh had gotten a Dangerous Book for Boys manual for his tenth birthday and had proudly shown off the trap he built from the instructions. Of course, Alex had made it into an adventure. They had all built their own and set off to see who could catch the most fish. Quinn had won and they were completely grossed out when his grandma had made them all gut and clean the fish before she would cook them for the group. Emily looked at David and they started to laugh. They had the same memory of Josh dumping fish guts down Alex's back and how she had chased him all around the farm until he begged for mercy.

They shared their story with Mason and Lisa over a split package of hot ramen noodles and beef jerky. Lisa had a sad smile on her face when they finished the story.

"You guys are so lucky. You both have great friends and amazing memories. I wish I did." she said, looking down.

Emily reached over and grabbed her hand. "You do have great friends and we are making memories together every day."

Lisa smiled gratefully back. It was full dark and they were all tired from another long physical day but they had learned their lesson from the previous night and tonight there would be a watch posted. Emily was happy to take the first shift because it meant that she would get uninterrupted sleep after she was done. They would have to change the roster every night to make it fair. The sounds of the forest and her friend's soft breathing kept her company until she woke Mason to take over. As she closed her eyes she pictured Alex smacking Josh across the face with a dead fish in payback so she fell asleep with a smile on her face.

Chapter 24

The smell of cooking fish woke Emily and Lisa up that morning. She opened her eyes and looked at David who was tending the pan on the fire. When he saw her looking at him, he smiled.

"I figured you caught them so I should clean them! You did good, Em. There were two decent-sized ones in the trap. This is going to be a great day. There are two cups of hot water over there for you girls if you want to wash up. These bad boys will be ready in a few minutes and I made some rice to go with the fish."

Emily had to smile. It was a much better way to wake up than yesterday. Fish and rice to start the day sounded pretty good. She poured out some warm water on a cloth and scrubbed her face and arms. She and Lisa braided each other's hair to keep it out of the way and a quick rinse of their toothbrushes had them ready for the day. Even without seasoning, the fish was amazing and everyone scraped their plates clean. They all pitched in to clean up and used the nearby stream for washing.

Once all the backpacks were on and the bedrolls slung, they started north once again. They didn't really know where they were but they had to be close to crossing over the border. It was two hours into their third day of walking when they left a field and climbed onto a paved road. Emily's leg muscles thanked her for the even surface. Walking through muddy, hilly fields was hard work and climbing over fences was annoying. The road ran east so they walked into the sun. A glint of steel in the distance flashed at them now and again and as they got closer they saw it was an abandoned car. All of the doors were open and there was trash spread out around it. There was nothing they could use so they just leaned against the sun warmed metal and took a break.

Emily handed out some of the candy she had found back in the house they had searched and they all enjoyed the sugar rush. All the teens were feeling the effects of the food rationing. They were burning up a lot of calories walking all day but not replacing them. David was leaned over pulling wires from under the steering wheel and tossing them out onto the road. Once he had a small pile he climbed out and started to sort them by length. He wound them up into a ball and stuffed them into a side pocket of the back pack.

Mason was watching him with a frown. "What are you going to use those for?"

He smiled and looked at Emily. "Well, I can't let her do all the work feeding us. She'd never let me forget it," he said in a teasing way. "When we stop tonight I'll strip the plastic off the wires and set them up as snares. We should be able to catch a few small animals to stretch our food supply."

Mason was grinning in appreciation. "Wow, you really are a Boy Scout!"

David sent him a scowl. That was something that Mark had said as an insult and David didn't find it funny. When Mason saw the look, he quickly backtracked.

"No, no, really, it's awesome. You and Emily know all this...stuff to get food and water. It's really great. I just wish I could help too. I'm a total dead weight and I don't know anything that would help us." he said, looking down in regret.

David studied him for a minute before nodding. "Well, there are lots of things we could teach you. Don't feel bad, Mason. Emily and I have lived on farms our whole lives and we spent a lot of time camping and hunting. That wasn't a part of your upbringing so it's not your fault. Things are different now so watch and learn how to do these things and you will be just fine."

Before Mason could reply, Lisa called out. She was standing at the back of the car looking in to the open trunk.

"Hey, guys, come and look at this!" she called out excitedly.

The three of them went to the back of the car and looked into the trunk. There was nothing in it but a spare tire. They looked at a grinning Lisa and shrugged. She laughed in delight.

"Not in the trunk, under it!" And she pointed at the back end of the car.

It took Emily a minute to process what she was seeing but when she got it, she let out a whoop of joy. On the white rectangular licence plate were the words, Beautiful British Columbia. Somewhere, sometime, they had crossed into Canada. Even though they were still hundreds of miles from home, Emily felt a surge of hope. With a renewed determination, the group turned east and continued on their way.

They had no idea where exactly they were in the province but they were headed in the right direction. After an hour of walking, they came to some railway tracks that were headed north. The group decided to follow them and it made for easier walking. They followed the tracks through many fields with distant homes visible but kept walking. When they saw that the tracks were headed to a built-up area they left them and turned east. The mountains were in front of them and they got closer with every step.

Emily knew that they would have to hit a main highway to get over them. There was no way they could travel through the mountains unless they followed the highway. Traveling on the main roads meant towns and people. She knew there were a lot of good people in the world but after their previous experiences, she would rather just avoid everyone. They camped that night in another clearing and dinner was one granola bar and one strip of beef jerky each. David and Mason stripped the plastic from the wires and David showed him how to set them up. They all hoped for something to eat in the morning.

The next morning started off bad and went downhill from there. It had started raining in the night and they were all wet and cold. They had left their camp in the clearing and moved deeper into the woods but the rain came through and they huddled together for warmth. When David had checked his traps he was disappointed to find them empty. So breakfast was some water and the last of the jerky. It was too wet to try and start a fire so they just stayed under their meager shelter and waited for the cold spring rain to pass. Being under trees didn't keep all the rain off of them but they needed any shelter they could find. After two hours, the rain became a drizzle and the dark clouds moved further away.

They came out from under the tree they had sheltered under and stretched their cramped muscles. It was time to move on and they could only hope that the sun would come out to dry their drenched clothes. Lisa and Emily headed deeper into the woods to find some privacy to go to the bathroom. They had only gone twenty feet when they stumbled out onto a wide trail. What shocked them the most was the two men who were also on the trail leaning against two quads. The men were just as surprised to see the girls and their mouths hung open in shock.

Emily eyed them warily and moved closer to Lisa. It didn't take the men long to overcome their surprise and they both stood and looked the girls up and down with big grins. The first man to speak was big and rough looking. He had dirty greasy hair and a bushy beard.

"Well, looky here, Wayne. We've got ourselves some company!" He gave his friend a knowing leer. "I bet we could have some fun with them!"

Wayne was smaller than his friend but looked just as rough and his brown eyes were cold.

"What about the others? Should we take them back to camp?"

"Hell no! They're at least ten miles from here. Why would we want to share? They don't even have to know!"

Lisa clutched Emily's arm while the two animals talked about them like they weren't even there. Her face was bone white and her eyes held pure terror. Lisa knew exactly what these men planned to do to them. She took a step back and a whimper escaped her lips when Emily stood stock-still. The tall man glanced over at Lisa and his face split into an amused grin.

"That's good, sweetheart, I like it when they cry." He took a menacing step towards them and then flew backwards and toppled over his quad.

Emily had no memory of pulling the gun from her pocket but when the shot man's friend bellowed in rage, she swung it towards him and pulled the trigger again. The shot caught him in the shoulder and twisted him sideways so he was leaning on his machine. Emily stood frozen watching as he pushed himself up off of it and turned to her with hate-filled eyes. He opened his mouth to speak but before he could she pulled the trigger for the third time and his face disappeared.

Someone was screaming. Emily hadn't moved and she stared straight ahead where the ugly man's face had been. She was unaware of the rain and tears mixing and flowing down her face. She didn't hear David and Mason's frantic yells for them or feel the ache in her hand that continued to clutch the cold, heavy gun. It was only when David tried to take it from her that she finally came back into herself. She yanked her hand and the gun away from him and clutched it to her chest. The scream that came out of her made the others freeze and stare at her in horror. It contained all the fear, rage and hopelessness of a broken soul. She fell to her knees and rocked back and forth on the muddy trail.

"Why, why, why?" she wailed in a pitiful voice.

David looked down at the girl he loved and his heart broke. All he wanted was to gather her up in his arms and hold her and keep her safe but he was afraid to touch her. He looked around at the others and saw Lisa staring blankly at the ground. Both of the girls were in shock and he didn't know what to do. Mason was checking the men's bodies so David went to help him. They were both dead and he had to force the vomit back down when he saw the one man's face. He helped Mason pull the bodies off the trail and into the woods. Both of the men were wearing camouflage rain slickers so their bodies weren't visible after the boys threw some branches on top of them. It was grisly work but he knew that Emily wouldn't have shot them if they were good people. He didn't know what had happened on the trail but when they heard the gun going off in the direction the girls had gone, he tore through the trees with no thought but getting to Emily.

When the two boys made it back to the trail, Lisa had Emily up and was holding her tight. The gun was gone. David didn't know who had it but he was relieved that it was no longer clutched in her hand. David stepped towards them but Mason stopped him with a shake of his head. So they checked over the two machines and the supplies strapped onto the back of them. There was food and water but not a lot. Both had an extra fuel can strapped down but what they didn't find was any guns. David was sure that the men would have rifles or shot guns but other than a sharp hunting knife, there were no other weapons.

Lisa's urgent voice had them both spinning around. "We have to get out of here, out of the woods! They said there are others in a camp. We need to get away from here in case they show up!"

Mason and David looked at each other in concern and they both tried to start the quads. When they started up right away they shut them off and Mason helped Lisa get Emily on one. David made a mad dash back to where they had left their things when they had bolted to find the girls. It didn't take long to gather the backpacks and get back to the trail. Mason helped strap them down and when he went to get on the quad that Emily was sitting on, David grabbed his arm.

"No, she's riding with me," he said with fierceness.

Mason looked at him in confusion until understanding dawned. He slowly nodded his head.

"Okay, man. Take care of her."

David nodded curtly and climbed on in front of Emily. He reached back and pulled her arms around him so she wouldn't fall off. When he felt her hand grip his waist, he closed his eyes for a minute. He almost lost her. All this time he had been sitting back and waiting for her to figure it out and he almost lost her. No more. He wasn't waiting any more. He loved her and he was going to make sure that she knew it.

They started the machines up and drove down the trail. When they came to an opening in the forest they could see a road in the distance so they left the trail and headed for it. David and Mason had decided to travel the roads from now on. They would make much better time and distance and they would need to be close to abandoned cars to siphon gas along the way. Once they were on the road, they increased their speed and made twenty miles in the first hour. It was right about then that Emily started to sob into his back and he knew she was coming out of her shock. The only thing he could do was briefly squeeze her hand and keep going.

They eventually connected with a bigger road and turned north onto it. There were more and more cars and trucks abandoned on the road but nothing they couldn't get around. To David, it felt like they were flying after walking for three days.

After two and a half hours and seventy miles, they stopped to refill the gas tanks from the spare cans. At the next group of abandoned cars, they stopped again and they took turns siphoning gas into the cans. They didn't want to take a chance and lose the precious vehicles. By the time the sun was going down behind them, they had gone a huge distance and they started to look for somewhere they could stop for the night. It was almost dark when they came to an old gas station that had been abandoned even before the lights went out. After carefully checking that no one was around, they forced the garage door open, and pushed the quads through.

It was dirty and dusty but it was dry and out of the wind. Emily hadn't spoken all day but she was more alert and followed Lisa into the small bathroom where they changed into the dry clothes from their packs. When the girls came out Emily looked much better and she had some color in her face. She gave David a small smile as she passed him and settled down on to the floor. Lisa took one of the few dry blankets and wrapped it around her before hanging the wet ones to dry. As the boys changed into dryer clothing, she started to go through the men's supplies.

Her hands had stopped shaking hours ago but she was chilled to the bone and she knew it wasn't just from the rain. Emily had saved them from being used and murdered but the callous way the men had talked about it had damaged her. Is this what they had to look forward to in this new world? Women having only one value and then discarded? She remembered what Mark had said back on the boat. He had said that only the strong would survive and they would take what they wanted. She looked up as David came into the room in dry clothes. The look he sent Emily was so full of love and concern that it hurt her heart a little bit that no one had ever looked at her that way. She turned away so no one would see the tears in her eyes. Was she that unlovable? Even her own parents had only ever shown her approval, never love.

She flinched when Mason came over and put his hand on her back. He quickly pulled away and his face reddened.

"I'm sorry. I just wanted to see if you were okay," he said quietly.

She nodded her head without looking at him and opened another bag from the back of the quad. It had six cans of chilli and beef stew in it. At the bottom of the bag was a small folding camp stove with a can of steno oil. She glanced over at Emily but David had sat down beside her and she had her head on his chest while he smoothed her hair. It was so obvious that David was in love with her and the only person who didn't seem to know was Emily.

Lisa turned away and carried the bag to a workbench. She studied the stove until she figured out how to set it up and then looked at Mason.

"Do you have any matches or a lighter?"

"Uh, no, but let me check in the other room and see if I can find something."

It was dark and gloomy with the overcast sky so he took a flashlight and went over to the sales counter and started to look around behind it. While he searched, Lisa got the pan from her pack and dumped two cans of beef stew into it. She hoped Mason found something because the cold stew wasn't very appetizing, looking like lumpy brown Jello in the bottom of the pot. She filled the other pot with water after she discovered a small jar of instant coffee in one of the other bags on the quad. Mason came over grinning and held up an old dried out book of matches. She waved him forward and he tried to light one of the matches. It was so old that it just crumbled, and it took four tries before one of them caught. Lisa sighed in relief and set the pan of stew on the stove.

The little stove warmed the pan quickly and the smell of the heating stew filled the garage. David and Emily stood up and came over. They found two bowls and spoon in the bags. They would have to take turns with them but they were just happy to have a hot meal. Once everyone had eaten and coffee had been made in the two travel mugs they found, they settled down and passed the hot drink back and forth between them.

David looked around the abandoned building. "Anyone know where we are?"

Mason perked up. "Yes, actually, I do. There's still an old map taped on the front wall in the other room. Someone circled an area in red and wrote "you are here" on it. We somehow got around Hope and we are now on the Coquihalla Highway. It looks like we are about a hundred miles to Merritt."

Emily jerked up and turned to David with a look of surprise. He slowly smiled and nodded.

Mason looked at Lisa in confusion but she just shrugged so he asked. "What, what's so special about Merritt?"

Emily just closed her eyes and breathed out, "Peter."

David laughed at her dramatics and explained, "Peter is Alex's older brother. He's an RCMP officer and that's where he is stationed. It would be really nice to see a familiar face right about now."

"Wow, that's great! Do you think he will help us?" Lisa asked hopefully.

"Oh, yeah, Peter might as well be my big brother. I've been driving him nuts with Alex since we were five!" Emily told her.

Emily was looking so happy but suddenly the smile melted off her face and her eyes filled with tears.

"Oh, my God! What am I going to tell him? I... I just killed two men! What...how...?"

Lisa was the quickest to react. She slid over and grabbed Emily's arm and shook it.

"Well, we better tell him about me too then! I killed Mark so he can deal with both of us!" she said fiercely.

Emily's mouth dropped open in shock. "What? That was self defence, Lisa. You saved us all!"

Lisa nodded and loosened her hold on Emily's arm. "So what do you think happened today? They talked about what they were going to do to us. We both know what would have happened if you hadn't shot them. Emily...you once told me that I had done the right thing and that I was a hero. Now I'm telling you the same thing. You saved us this time." Lisa sat back and let the tears fall. The tension went out of Emily and she reached out and pulled Lisa to her.

As the girls wept, David and Mason looked at each other. They didn't know what had happened on the trail today but they were both grateful that the girls had made it out alive. Mason was surprised at how he felt at the possibility of losing Lisa. He was so ashamed of the hurt he had caused her and every day on the road, she impressed him with her new determination and attitude. He had never seen her as anything other than a shallow cheerleader but she was so much more. He wished he could change things between them. He wished she would give him another chance.

They settled down for the night in the cold garage. With most of their blankets wet, they all huddled together and tried to sleep hoping that the next day would bring them closer to home and family.

Chapter 25

The sun was out to wake them the next morning and they were all happy to see clear skies. They decided to forego breakfast and just drank some hot coffee to start their day. Emily was anxious to get going. More than anything she wanted to find Peter, the closest thing she had to a brother. She wouldn't let herself think of all the things that could have happened to him since the lights went out. He was a cop and he would have been in danger from the very start.

As they traveled the famous highway north, they saw a lot of wildlife. Deer and elk wandered freely across the road and weaved in between the stranded vehicles. The cars were spread out and there were a lot of transport trucks on this road. A huge dual-trailered Safeway truck had jackknifed into the ditch and they stopped to see if they could get into it. There were padlocks on both trailers and they were sealed up tight. David looked around until he found the mile marker and memorised it. The kids might not be able to get in to the grocery truck but the people of Merritt could come and get it open.

What they didn't see was people. There were campgrounds and recreation areas along the highway but not a lot of residences. Anyone who had been stranded on this road would have walked out a long time ago. It had been twenty-four days since the world changed and most people would have made it to where they were going by now.

The highway mileage signs counted down the distance to their destination and they had to keep slowing down to a safe speed as their excitement got the better of them. Even in the excitement to get to Merritt, it was impossible not to be in awe of the amazing scenery they were passing. There were mountains, lakes, valleys and meadows filled with new spring growth all around them. The peaks still had snow on them and the clean air filled their lungs. It was one of the most beautiful places on earth and it inspired a peaceful feeling in all the teens.

The Coquihalla Highway was beautiful in spring and summer but was dubbed the Highway through Hell in the winter. It twisted and turned with the land and avalanches happened often. There were tunnels in the highest danger areas that would protect travelers from the rushing slides of death. The road didn't go through the town they were heading towards but circled around.

They came to the exit for the town in the early afternoon and as they made their way off the highway they could see the huge visitor center ahead of them and, for the first time since they got the quads, people. As they got closer they could make out four men and a woman sitting in lawn chairs around a fire in the middle of the parking lot. When the people heard the engines of the quads, they got up and walked towards them. One man raised his arm and waved. The people were all armed but the rifles stayed slung on their backs or shoulders and no one seemed hostile.

As the teens came to a stop at the entrance to the parking lot, one man stepped towards them and Emily could see he was wearing an RCMP uniform. She smiled a huge smile at him and removed her hand from her pocket. She had been clutching the gun tight. There was only one bullet left but she would make it count if she had too.

He looked them over with a nod.

"Hello! Where are you kids heading?"

Emily took the lead. "We were hoping to head into town. My best friend's brother lives here and we were hoping to find him."

"Sure, you guys head on in. If you don't find him, there are two refugee camps setup and anyone in town will direct you. If you kids are planning on staying, there's a registration desk there and they will get you set up with food and housing." The officer smiled at their looks of disbelief.

Lisa asked him tentatively, "Is it safe?"

He gave her a sad smile. "Yes, it is. We have a small population and when the Event happened, most everyone stayed calm. We had a few bad apples that started some trouble but we put them down fast. Most people here are used to losing power so we have a lot of generators and the hunting around here is pretty good so food wasn't much of an issue. I take it you kids have seen some trouble?"

Before they could answer the woman came over and handed out travel mugs she had filled from the pot on the campfire. The teens smile gratefully and sipped at the hot chocolate in the mugs. The woman looked them over with compassion.

"How far have you come?"

The shocked looks on their faces were comical when Emily said, "California."

The officer sputtered. "What...how? There's no way!"

Emily and the others nodded with serious faces and she explained where they had been and how they had come so far. The people just stared at them in awe so she kept talking.

"We live in central Alberta so after we find Peter, we plan on continuing on."

The officer just shook his head in amazement. His eyes narrowed at a thought and he asked.

"Wait a minute. You kids were on a class trip to Disneyland and you're all from Alberta?"

When they nodded, his face broke in to a grin. "You're looking for Pete Andrews, aren't you?" he asked in disbelief.

Emily leaned forward. "Yes! How do you know that? Do you know him?" She was almost vibrating with excitement as the officer started to laugh.

"Yes, I know him, we work together. He told me a while back about his sister being in California. He assumed she didn't make it, a city that size would have exploded with violence. You said she was your best friend. Is she with you guys?" He looked at Lisa questioningly and she shook her head.

The woman stepped forward and handed a radio to the officer. "Bill, call down to the station and get Pete up here. He can lead them to his place."

He took the radio and stepped away to make the call. The woman waved them over to the campfire so the kids left the quads and went to stand around the fire, warming their hands.

"When was the last time you kids ate?" she asked with a frown.

David smiled at her concern. "We had a hot supper last night but nothing today, ma'am."

She quickly opened a cooler and pulled out a plastic container of sandwiches. After thanking her, they all devoured them. A thick slice of venison roast on freshly baked bread with spicy mustard was heaven to the kids and they all groaned in pleasure at the taste.

Emily couldn't keep her eyes from the road to town and she paced back and forth waiting for Peter to get there. She was dreading having to tell him about Alex. While they waited, David told them about the sealed up Safeway truck and were they could find it. The four of them were happy to hear about it and the woman started making calls on the radio. When the sound of a motor finally reached her ears, she stood frozen and watched Peter come tearing into the parking lot. He had barely come to a stop before he was out the door and running towards her. The look of joy on his face was all it took for her to launch herself at him and his big arms wrapped around her and swung her in a circle. He was laughing as he set her down and looked at her tear-covered face. He planted a huge kiss on her forehead and then looked at the other kids that were standing watching the reunion. Peter grinned at David and nodded at Mason and Lisa but his eyes were searching the parking lot for his sister. When he didn't find her he looked down at Emily with confusion.

"Em...where's Alex?"

Emily's face crumpled. Looking at him was like looking at Alex. They both had the same strawberry blond hair and green eyes. It made it even harder to tell him. "Oh, Peter, I don't know! I'm sorry, I'm so sorry!" she wailed. He pulled her back into his arms and held her tight.

"It's okay, it's okay," he soothed her. As Emily sobbed in Peter's strong arms, David told him what happened and how they had split up.

"She's with Quinn and Josh and a few others so they are probably home by now."

Peter nodded and gave a half-hearted laugh. "Oh man, I can just imagine the trail of destruction that group will have left behind!" he joked. "Okay, let's get you guys to my place. Susan will help you get settled. I need to get back to work but we can talk about our next steps over supper when I get home." Emily went in the truck with Peter so they could talk while the others followed behind on the Quads.

"How is Susan? Did she have the baby yet?" Emily asked him. She didn't know Peter's wife very well. He had met her in Lethbridge where he had been posted when he had first started in the RCMP. His wife had visited their hometown a few times before their wedding but they had spent most of their time with Peter and Alex's parents. She was pregnant with their first child and was due at any moment.

Peter smiled. "No, her due date is still two weeks away. She's been pretty tired and our doctor wants her to take it easy. I thought about going home to Prairie Springs after the Event but with her so close to delivering, I felt it was safer to stay put. I think the hardest part of this whole thing is the not knowing. It's driving me crazy not knowing what's going on at home." He glanced at her and smiled. "I've been so worried about Alex, but even though we don't know if she made it home, I feel a lot better knowing that they tried to get out of that city. I can't imagine how bad it was but if they took off right away, they had a good chance of making it."

Emily watched the town slide by and was amazed at how calm everything was. A lot of front lawns had been dug up and were ready to be planted for gardens. There were many tree stumps with piles of cut logs in a lot of driveways. There were plenty of people out walking in the spring sun and she even saw a few mothers pushing strollers. It was almost like the town hadn't been touched by the new world.

Peter kept talking as they drove to his house. "After the baby is born, I want to give Susan a month or so to recover and then we can all travel to Alberta together."

Emily looked back out the window at the peaceful town and considered staying here safe and sound for the next two months. It sounded like heaven but she knew they couldn't do it. Her parents had no idea where she was or even if she was alive and the others all had family to get home to as well.

"Thanks for offering to let us stay, Peter, but we need to get home. We will probably want to get going in a day or two."

Peter looked at her as if she were crazy. "Are you kidding me? It's almost eight hundred kilometers from here to home. There's no way I can let you kids travel that far alone. It's way too dangerous!"

Emily just tilted her head and stared at him in silence until he glanced away from the street ahead and looked at her.

"What?" he asked in confusion.

"Peter, how far is it from California to here?" When he didn't respond, only looked back at the street and frowned she went on. "It's a lot further than eight hundred kilometers. We have been traveling alone for twenty-four days. I know exactly how dangerous it is out there. I've lived through it!"

The last was said with bitterness and Peter looked at her sharply. "Did something happen out there? Did someone hurt you, Emily?"

She could only shake her head and look away. The rest of the drive was in silence and they were soon at his home. As they were getting out of the truck, the front door opened and a very pregnant Susan came down the steps. Peter made the introductions and they all went into the house. Peter kissed his wife and told her briefly what had happened to the teens before leaving to go back to work. Susan was very gracious to them and she showed them where they could sleep. They had a generator so there was hot water for a few showers and Peter had set up a solar shower in the back yard as well. The boys offered to use the solar one and the girls raced each other to the bathroom. It felt amazing to be clean and even better to have clean clothes when Susan offered some of her pre-pregnancy clothes.

Emily felt amazing. They were safe and clean with the closest thing to family she could find. She and Lisa helped Susan prepare for supper and the simple normal task of peeling potatoes and carrots made her smile. By the time Peter returned from work, the house was filled with the smell of roast venison and baking bread. They were all sitting in the living room sharing stories with Susan and it was the most relaxed any of them had felt in almost a month.

When Peter joined them he sat beside his wife on the couch and leaned over to kiss her large belly. When he addressed them, it was in a serious tone.

"Emily said that you guys want to keep going in the next day or so. I just want to ask again if you would consider staying until after Susan has the baby and we can join you." When they all shook their heads, he went on. "I understand you want to go home but you've already been through so much and it scares me to think of you leaving alone. So, I put out some feelers and got some information. There is a group of people leaving here tomorrow in a convoy. They are headed up to Kamloops and then east on the Trans Canada to Golden. Some of them are stopping in places along the way, but four trucks plan to keep going and head up to Jasper. It doesn't get any better than that. They would drop you off at the Highway 11 junction and from there it's a straight shot home. The junction to town is only about a hundred and fifty kilometers so on the quads it shouldn't take you more than a day. Two of the trucks going are pulling toy hauler campers and they agreed to take you guys for some trade goods I put together."

Emily sprang across the room and hugged Peter. "We can't thank you enough! Oh, Peter…two days and we will be home! Thank you, thank you!"

He studied her face in seriousness. "I don't know what happened to you out there, Emily, but from this point on I want to make sure you are safe." He looked at the others. "I want all of you to be safe. So…who's ready for supper? It smells like it's done!"

Dinner was amazing and there was even enough for second helpings. Emily groaned from her stretched belly. None of them were used to eating so much after days of rationing. After the dishes were washed and put away they all settled around the coffee table for a game of Monopoly. There was a lot of laughter and Emily was surprised to realize how much she missed laughing. There had hardly been any reason to laugh since they left California.

The night wound down and when Susan went to bed the others followed quickly. They would have an early start in the morning and they wanted to get a good night's rest. Emily and Lisa were sharing the queen-sized bed in the guest room and the boys were on the pull-out couch. It felt so good to lay down on a soft mattress with clean sheets and Emily figured she would fall asleep right away.

Two hours later, she was still awake staring at the ceiling. Her mind was on overload with thoughts of home and her parents. She finally gave up and got dressed. She quietly slipped out of the room so she wouldn't wake Lisa up and crept through the house to the back door. She grabbed one of Peter's jackets hanging by the door and went out to sit on the back patio.

The night was cold and crisp and beautiful. She let herself go back and retrace the whole trip in her head. All the horrible things that had happened and the things she had seen flashed through her mind. She was a different person than the girl that left Disneyland. They all were. Mason and Lisa had changed so much from the people they had been and she was glad that she could call Lisa a friend now. And David, he had always been a good friend but she saw him differently now. He was so much more than a friend and she wasn't sure what that meant.

As if her thoughts had summoned him, he came out of the house and sat down on the bench beside her.

"Are you okay?" he asked softly.

She smiled and took his hand in hers. "Yes, I was just thinking and looking at the stars. They're so beautiful, aren't they?"

He squeezed her hand and said, "Yes, beautiful."

When she looked at him, he wasn't looking at the stars but at her. She felt her cheeks redden and she looked down at her lap in embarrassment.

"I'm an idiot, right?" she whispered.

He laughed and tilted her head up so she was looking at him. "Yes, but so am I for waiting so long." He took a deep breath and stared deep into her eyes. "I've loved you since you had pigtails, Emily Clarkson, and I've waited all this time for you to notice. I almost lost you yesterday so I'm not going to wait anymore."

"Oh, David, I'm sorry I was so blind," she said sadly.

He was very serious when he said, "It's okay. I know how you can make it up to me."

When she raised her eyebrows in a question, he leaned forward and kissed her. It was the sweetest, most meaningful kiss of her whole life. Emily's body lit up with love and hope. This was where she was supposed to be and this was the boy she was supposed to be with. When they pulled apart, they both had tears in their eyes and they held onto each other. David and Emily had spent almost every day together growing up and they knew that they would spend the rest of their lives together too.

Chapter 26

Emily looked down the line of trucks, an antique school bus and two antique cars that were parked at the visitor's center. The owners of the toy haulers were finishing strapping down the quads and they were almost ready to go. They had already put their backpacks and extra supplies that Peter and Susan had given them in the front of the camper and all that was left was to say goodbye.

She turned to Peter and he handed her a letter to give to his parents. "Tell them we will be there in two months, in plenty of time to help with the harvest. Mom better get busy making cloth diapers because we will be out of disposable ones by then!" He pulled her in for a hug. "Be safe, Emily. Be careful and give my sister a kiss for me when she shows up."

Her voice was too choked with tears to say anything so she just hugged him harder. David came up and shook Peter's hand. Everyone thanked him again for all his help and then they were climbing into the trailer and pulling away.

The trip to Golden was the easiest day of travel since they had come ashore. They sat at the dinette and played cards while the miles passed them by. The convoy stopped at quite a few towns on the way but only long enough to get out and stretch their legs and say good bye to one of the vehicles that were stopping and then they moved on. When they finally got to Golden, it was just before supper and the four trucks filled with families set up the trailers and started BBQs. It all seemed to go so fast to Emily and she couldn't believe that they were down to hours before they would be home. She expected to have trouble sleeping again but within minutes of crawling into one of the trailer's bunk beds she was gone.

Hot cereal and canned fruit was served at dawn for breakfast. With no electricity, people had started to get up with the sun and go to bed early. With everyone pitching in to clean up, they were on the road by seven. The teens weren't used to traveling so fast after days of walking so they were all surprised when they felt the trucks slow down and stop. When they opened the camper door, the first thing they saw was the highway sign for the exit to Highway 11 and Prairie Springs.

Emily jumped down on to the road and ran over to it. She reached up and ran her hand over the name of her hometown.

"So close," she thought to herself and spun around to smile at her friends.

It didn't take the men long to unstrap and unload the quads and after much thanks and hugs and handshakes, the small group of teens stood and watched the trucks drive away. When they couldn't see the trucks anymore, they climbed on to the machines and made the turn east. As they drove down the road that would take them home, they were all smiling.

They had to stop and fill the gas tanks a few hours later and even though they wanted to hurry, they took the time to siphon more gas so they would have full spare gas cans. No one wanted to stop to make food so they ate as they drove and kept it to deer jerky and granola bars. Emily's cheeks hurt from smiling at every landmark she recognised.

They were coming up to the access road to the lake and all the RV resorts when two old pickup trucks pulled on to the highway and blocked the road ahead. It was only twenty minutes to town from there so they all assumed that they were townspeople on security. The teens stopped the quads and got off. They were all grinning and trying to see if they recognized anyone when four loud motorcycles drove around the trucks and stopped.

Emily felt a shiver run down her back. Something was wrong here. None of the men looked like they were from her town and when they got off their bikes, they pointed rifles and shotguns at them as they advanced. The looks the men were giving her and Lisa confirmed that they were in big trouble.

A man with long greasy hair and dirty yellow teeth stepped ahead of the others and gave them a huge smile. He zeroed in on Emily and she shrank back from his cold, reptilian eyes.

"Hello, pretty girl! So nice of you to come to our party and you brought a friend!" His rough voice oozed fake charm.

Emily lifted her chin and swallowed the lump in her throat. "Who are you?" she asked cautiously.

He kept walking towards her and stopped when he was a few feet away. Still smiling, he gave her an exaggerated bow but when he came up from it he was no longer smiling and he had a handgun pointed at her head.

"Let's just say I'm the Prairie Springs Welcoming committee. You and your girlfriend are welcome. The boys...not so much! Get into the truck!" he roared the last command.

Emily was frozen. What was going on here? What was happening in her town? Who were these animals? The man made an ugly face at her and cocked his gun. He opened his mouth to yell at her again but before he could a voice called out from the ditch on the side of the road.

"I'm pretty sure she doesn't want to go anywhere with someone as ugly as you!" the voice taunted.

Emily's eyes flew wide. That voice, she had known that voice all her life. Her head turned as if in slow motion and there she was. Her red gold curls gleamed in the sun and she stood tall and fierce with the biggest gun Emily had ever seen pointed right at the nasty man.

He swivelled around and moved his gun so it was pointing at Alex. "Well, what do you know? Look guys, we got another pretty little girl to join the party!" and he laughed.

A voice from the other side of the road called out. "Hey! It's really stupid to tease a redhead with a big gun, mister. If I was you, I'd duck and cover 'cause she looks pissed!"

Emily knew that was Josh yelling out and she wondered who else was hidden around the road. The long

~ 204 ~

haired man kept his eyes on Alex the whole time but his mouth moved in to a smirk.

"Don't worry, buddy, she'll be playing with my big gun soon enough!"

Emily was looking at Alex and her heart was pounding. Every childhood memory flashed before her eyes. Every adventure they had shared every secret they had giggled over was right there. "That's my sister!" she thought as she pulled the gun from her pocket and with her last bullet shot the man threatening her.

As gunshots filled the air around her she felt herself being thrown to the ground as David tackled her and covered her body with his. As her head slammed into the hard pavement, her last thoughts before darkness took her was, "This is wrong. We don't have to fight any more. We are HOME."

To Be Continued…End of Book Two

Coming Soon

City - A Stranded Novella

Mrs. Moore and the rest of the students that remained in California face the harsh reality that no one is coming to help them. As the city burns around them, they are surrounded by 18 million people with one goal…survival. Will Mrs. Moore's determination be enough to save them? Surrounded by chaos, they must work together to find a shelter before it's too late.

Home - A Stranded Novel

Five went by Land and five went by Sea. Nine made it through the chaos Home. With their town under siege, and their families both prisoners and slaves, they will have the biggest challenge yet. After witnessing the pain and suffering in the town, the group of teens have to decide just how far they are willing to go to save them. Life sucks when you are Home, but still Stranded.

Made in the USA
San Bernardino, CA
27 May 2015